SCENT OF DANGER

A CHRISTIAN ROMANTIC SUSPENSE

SULLIVAN K9 SEARCH AND RESCUE

LAURA SCOTT

Copyright © 2024 by Laura Iding

All rights reserved.

No part of this book may be reproduced in any form or by any electronic or mechanical means, including information storage and retrieval systems, without written permission from the author, except for the use of brief quotations in a book review.

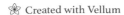 Created with Vellum

1

His half sister was late.

DEA Agent Doug Bridges nursed his coffee, trying to ignore the shiver of apprehension sliding down his spine as he stared out the window of the Hitching Post Café in Cody, Wyoming. Emily had recently moved to the area from Jackson and worked night shift as a nurse in the emergency department, so there was no reason to panic. One of her patients could have crashed in the middle of shift change.

Yet it was nearly forty-five minutes since their designated meeting time. The interior of the café was warm, especially compared to the outside temperature of a whopping 12 degrees. He was glad the snow had stopped after blanketing the town with two inches of fluff the night before. Now the sun was trying to peek out from behind the clouds that hung over the Bighorn Mountains.

For what seemed like the hundredth time, he glanced at his silent phone, willing it to ring. It didn't. He finally picked it up and called Emily, hoping she'd say she was on her way.

Straight to voice mail.

The niggling concern grew. He finished his coffee and pulled some cash from his pocket to cover the tab. Sitting in the café wasn't helping. He was supposed to head to the Yellowstone Regional Airport to catch his flight that would take him through Denver, then home to Milwaukee, Wisconsin. Emily wouldn't miss their last meal together without a good reason.

Doug shrugged into his thick winter coat and drew on a woolen hat and thick gloves. He hadn't expected Wyoming to be that much colder than Wisconsin, but he'd underestimated the impact of the mountains and the wind.

He left the Hitching Post and slid in behind the wheel of his four-wheel drive rental SUV. He'd head over to the hospital to meet Emily. If there was time, they could grab a bite in the cafeteria. He didn't want to leave without saying goodbye. Having worked with the Finnegans and the Callahans over the past few years, he'd decided to mend his relationship with his family.

Hence spending the Christmas and New Year holidays with his half sister Emily.

The drive to the local medical center didn't take long. The hospital was located on the far west side of town, and they'd purposefully chosen the Hitching Post as a meeting spot because it was halfway between the medical facility and his hotel.

The parking lot was only half full, and when he saw Emily's Jeep covered in a two-inch layer of snow, he relaxed. Good to know she was still working. He pulled into the open space next to hers and shut down the engine. Hunching his shoulders against the chill, he stood for a moment, glancing around the area, then strode inside the emergency department entrance.

The waiting room was empty except for two people

who were hacking up half a lung. Feeling bad for them, he went to the front desk. A plump woman who was old enough to be his grandmother glanced up at him expectantly. Her name tag identified her as Barbara. "May I help you?"

He smiled. "Hi, I'm Emily's brother Doug Bridges. Can you let her know I'm waiting for her?"

Barbara frowned. "Emily left almost an hour ago."

The niggling concern billowed into full-fledged alarm. "What do you mean? Her car is still out in the parking lot."

"It is?" Barbara appeared flustered. "I don't understand. Emily waved at me as she left, explaining how she was meeting her brother for breakfast at the Post. I don't think she'd walk to the café in this weather."

No, she wouldn't. Doug instantly went into federal agent mode. "I want to talk to someone in charge, and I need to see your video camera footage."

Barbara's eyes widened, and she reached for the phone. "Stan? You better get out here. Seems as if Emily might be missing."

Stan strode toward him a long minute later. He was in his mid-fifties and was wearing what appeared to be a security officer uniform. "I'm Stan Turner, the security officer for the hospital. You're Emily's brother?"

"Yes, Doug Bridges." He shook Stan's hand, briefly wondering if the entire hospital staff knew his sister. "I need to see your camera footage. Barbara saw Emily leave, but her car is still outside in the parking lot. And she didn't meet me for breakfast as planned."

Stan hesitated for a moment as if deciding whether he should comply, then nodded. "Okay. Follow me."

His small office was located just beyond the waiting area. It took the older man so long to pull up the video it was all

Doug could do not to thrust him aside to figure it out for himself.

"Okay, Emily's shift would have ended at seven thirty," Stan said. He poked at the keyboard, then used the mouse. "Here she is."

Doug wedged himself behind the desk so he could see the computer screen. His gut tightened when he saw Emily waving at Barbara, seemingly saying something as she headed toward the main entrance. His sister was wearing her cherry-red parka coat, her blond hair was covered by a matching red hat, and she was wearing cherry-red gloves. Within seconds, she went through the automatic doors and disappeared around the corner, seemingly toward the parking lot.

"Okay, can you switch to one of the outside cameras?" Doug asked. "You must have one that overlooks the parking lot."

"We do," Stan agreed. He pulled up two more cameras before finding the right one. He fast-forwarded to match the time frame of the previous camera. Then he hit the play button.

There was nothing. No sign of Emily crossing the parking lot to her car.

"Back it up," Doug said, feeling grim. "Maybe the clocks between the cameras don't match."

"They match," Stan protested. "They're on the same system." But he did as Doug asked, backing up the video to a full five minutes earlier. The silence hung heavy as they watched as nobody walked past for a full fifteen minutes. That's when a car pulled into the lot, and one of the coughing patients got out and came inside.

That was it. No sign of Emily. Or anyone else, which he found odd. He frowned, staring at Stan. "Okay, pull up the cameras facing the other way. Maybe she saw someone she knew and went over to speak with them."

Stan flushed. "We don't have cameras overlooking the street. We only have them covering the main entrance, the emergency department entrance, and the parking lot."

Three cameras? Really? "Okay, bring up the main entrance." He tried not to show his frustration. Milwaukee wasn't anywhere near as large as Chicago, Detroit, or Minneapolis, but he happened to know that Trinity Medical Center had over six hundred cameras covering the property. Three seemed ridiculous.

More seconds dragged by as Stan manipulated the screen. "Here we are," he finally said.

Several people could be seen using the main entrance, despite the early hour. But none of them were Emily.

"Maybe you oughta call the police," Stan said, his expression mirroring Doug's concerns. "Seems strange that Emily would vanish like that."

"Thanks. Would you please send me a copy of that emergency department video?" He hoped the security guard would cooperate, but if he didn't, Doug had no trouble using his badge to go over his head. "Please," he added. "That's Emily's last-known location. Proof that she left, at least originally, under her own power."

"Okay, where should I send it?" Stan asked.

Doug quickly provided his email address, waiting until the message had popped up on his phone before stepping back. "Thank you."

"Anytime," Stan said. "You know, before you head to the police department, you should make sure Emily didn't head home. Maybe she caught a ride with someone because she was having car trouble."

He nodded without pointing out that didn't make sense.

The camera would have shown Emily walking to her car, trying to start it, then coming back inside. Or walking to meet him at the café. Or calling him for a ride.

It was as if she'd stepped into an alternate universe, if you believed in that sort of thing.

He didn't. His earlier apprehension returned in full force. He walked back through the emergency department, trying not to think about how long Emily had been gone. A full hour by now, maybe a little more.

He hated knowing the trail had already grown cold—literally and figuratively.

Outside the emergency department, he paused to glance around. As before, he didn't see anything suspicious. Both corners of the building were out of camera range, so he turned toward the side of the building closest to the parking lot.

Forcing himself to stop and think, he took a moment to clear his mind. This was not the time to make a mistake. He stood back, slowly raking his gaze over the ground. His heart thumped when he noticed what appeared to be several footprints crisscrossing in the snow.

He scanned the length of the building, then looked up to locate the camera. When he found it, he grimly realized that anyone walking along the building itself would be able to stay out of sight.

A chill that had nothing to do with the freezing temperatures washed over him. Moving forward, he followed the side building until he reached the ambulance bay. Of course, there were no cameras overlooking that area.

He turned and retraced his steps, his thoughts whirling. In his mind's eye, he could imagine someone standing near the corner, maybe showing distress as that person asked Emily for help.

And then what? Kidnapped her?

It was hard to imagine anyone doing that, but what was the alternative? Doug hurried back to his rental, mentally making a list of tasks. Check Emily's house. Go to the local police department. Call his boss, Special Agent in Charge Donovan, to explain that he wouldn't be back to work as planned.

And from there? As a federal agent, he knew how to investigate crimes, specifically drug trafficking. But out here in the middle of small-town Wyoming, he was at a distinct disadvantage.

He'd need help from local experts. And soon.

Before Emily was hurt or killed.

MAYA SULLIVAN SLID out from behind the wheel of her specially designed K9 SUV and clicked the button to open the back. The door rose, but Zion, her Siberian husky, didn't jump down.

"Come, Zion," she said sternly. "You like Dr. Andrew, remember?"

Her K9 partner still didn't move. Suppressing a sigh, she moved closer to look directly into the blue eyes of her partner. "Out!"

Zion jumped down as if she'd been waiting for the magic word. This was a routine vet visit for Zion, and usually the husky was anxious and raring to go.

As she closed the back hatch, a voice came from behind her. "Ms. Sullivan?"

She whirled, her hand going to the pocket of her coat that held her gun. Recently, she'd caught a glimpse of someone following her, and suddenly there was a tall stranger standing there. Zion came over to stand protectively in front of her.

Seeing the dog, the stranger abruptly stopped. "Are you Maya Sullivan?"

She tried to relax. As the oldest of nine siblings residing on the Sullivan K9 Search and Rescue ranch, she was often called upon by strangers. Although usually not while she was in town visiting the vet. "Yes, I'm Maya, and this is Zion, my K9 partner. May I ask who you are?"

"Doug Bridges." A look of relief flashed in his eyes. "I've heard great things about you and your ranch, and I'm in desperate need of your expertise."

Maya dropped her hand from her pocket and resisted the urge to glance at her watch. She forced a smile. "I'm sorry, but Zion has a nine o'clock appointment inside. I'll be happy to chat with you when that's finished."

"No, I can't wait that long." Bridges took a step closer, causing Zion to growl low in her throat. He stopped where he was, his gaze beseeching. "Please. My sister, Emily Sanders, went missing at seven thirty-five this morning. She's a nurse and left the hospital after her night shift, then disappeared. I'm desperately in need of your search and rescue services."

"Emily? Emily Sanders is your sister?" She narrowed her gaze, eyeing him with suspicion. "Funny, the last time I saw Emily she didn't mention a brother."

"Half brother," he clarified. "I—we haven't really interacted with each other much until the past few months." A gust of cold wind hit hard, making her realize they were standing around in the freezing temperatures. "How do you know my sister?"

Maya wasn't in the mood to discuss how Emily had treated her youngest sister, Kendra, in the emergency department after a terrible fall. Her family's personal life was none of his concern. But knowing Emily was missing gave her pause. "Are you sure she's not at home? Or still working?"

His green eyes flared with anger, but he didn't yell or shout. "I'm sure. I've been to the hospital and have video of her leaving through the front entrance. But her car is still there, covered in snow from last night, and she never crossed the parking lot. I double-checked her house and went to the local police." Now his mouth tightened. "I've filed a missing person report, but the officer on duty basically told me I would be better off hiring someone from the Sullivan K9 Search and Rescue ranch than waiting for them to find her. I was about to head that way when I saw your car."

She didn't bother to glance at the SUV with the Sullivan K9 Search and Rescue logo stenciled along the side. That had been her brother Chase's bright idea, and lately, when she'd sensed someone following her, she'd been tempted to cover the lettering with paint.

Another cold blast of air convinced her that standing out here talking wasn't smart. And she couldn't walk away from this. Missing persons cases happened to be Zion's specialty. With a sigh, she nodded. "I'll help search for Emily. First, I need you to step closer."

His expression uncertain, he did as she asked. She put a hand on his arm. "Friend, Zion. Doug is a friend."

Zion sniffed his feet, then wagged her tail. Doug gave her a grateful look.

"Okay, now that Zion knows you're not the enemy, let's get back inside the SUV where it's warmer."

Doug didn't hesitate to open the passenger door. She clicked the fob to open the back and gave Zion the hand gesture to get inside. Zion tilted her head as if to ask, "Are you sure?" before jumping inside.

Sliding behind the wheel, she started the engine, then used her phone to call the vet. Easier to call to say she was out on a search than to do that in person. Thankfully, Dr. Andrew didn't mind her frequent need to reschedule. As she slid the gearshift into drive, she glanced at Doug. "You're not from this area, are you?"

He looked surprised. "No, why, is it that obvious?"

She smiled. "You speak with a distinct Midwest accent."

"Milwaukee, Wisconsin," he said. "I can pay you via credit card, a check, or cash. Whatever works for you."

She waved that off and turned to drive back to the hospital. Zion didn't stretch out to rest but kept her nose pressed to the crate as if intending to keep Doug Bridges in line. "Don't worry about payment. As far as searching for your sister, it's best if you have a scent source for her. Some sort of clothing. If that's not possible, Zion may be able to pick up her scent regardless, especially if I give her a few locations to work from. Can you tell me a little about Emily's personal life? Is she seeing someone?"

Doug seemed relieved to see the hospital looming on the horizon. He drew a pair of black gloves from his pocket. "These belong to Emily. I took them when I checked to make sure she hadn't gone home. To answer your question, Emily is not seeing anyone now that I'm aware of but did break up with her previous boyfriend roughly four months ago. That's one of the reasons she relocated from Jackson to Cody. She claimed Avery wasn't the least bit upset about the split, as he was planning to move to Colorado anyway. I guess he's some sort of ski instructor."

"Ah yes, Avery White," she said with a nod. "I'm not

surprised he left Wyoming for Colorado. He seemed to think he was destined for bigger things."

"Does everyone know everyone else in this town?" There was a sharp edge to his tone.

"For the most part, yes. Jackson is different. It's a resort town. I've done some skiing in the Tetons; Avery acted like he owned the place." Maya shot him a quick glance before she pulled into the parking lot. "Which car is Emily's?"

"That burgundy Jeep."

Seeing the vehicle, she nodded, then parked two spaces away. Keeping the engine on, she pulled a plastic bag from the glove box and carefully dropped Emily's gloves inside. "I'd like you to stay back to give Zion some room to work."

"Ms. Sullivan," he began.

"Maya," she quickly interjected. "We don't use formal titles around here."

"Okay, then call me Doug. I'm a federal agent with the DEA, and I would like to give you my working theory before you put Zion to work."

She held up a hand to stop him. "Really, it's better if you don't. I'm sure you're an excellent agent, but I won't go into this with preconceived ideas. We need to let Zion do her thing and go from there, okay?"

He frowned but nodded. "Okay."

While she found his career interesting, she wasn't going to let that interfere with how she and Zion worked together as a team. She released the back hatch, and this time, Zion eagerly jumped down. Zion's thick white-and-gray coat kept her warm during winter searches, and she held her curvy tail high as she sniffed the air.

As was her habit, Maya placed the vest over Zion's head, a physical indication they were going to work. Then she filled a bowl with water and set it down on the ground.

Water moistened the dog's mucus membranes, which enhanced her ability to follow scents. Zion only took two laps, then stared up at Maya with her pale-blue eyes, waiting for her next command.

"Good girl," Maya praised as she ran her fingers through Zion's thick gray-and-white coat. "Are you ready? Are you?" She liked to get the dog excited about the upcoming search. She opened the plastic bag containing Emily's gloves. "Emily," she said, giving the scent a name. She preferred using names on cases where they knew exactly who the victim was. "Search Emily."

Zion buried her snout deep into the bag for a long moment. Then she had her head up and was sniffing the air. Maya was far too aware of Doug standing beside the SUV, watching them work.

After a few seconds of sniffing, Zion whirled in a circle and bounded toward the burgundy Jeep. The K9 sniffed the ground around the car, then sat at the driver's side door and turned to stare intently up at Maya.

"Good girl," she praised, pulling a stuffed yellow bunny from her pocket. She tossed it into the air, and Zion leaped up to grab it. Then she shook her head back and forth, running in a circle as if oblivious to the frigid temps. Huskies loved to goof around.

Maya half expected Doug to protest the playtime, but he remained silent. Maybe his experience was such that he knew working dogs needed to be rewarded for a job well done. She waited for Zion to return to her side. "Hand," she said. With reluctance, Zion regurgitated the stuffed bunny in her gloved palm. "Good girl. Search. Search Emily."

Eager to get back to work, Zion sniffed the ground around the Jeep, then trotted toward the front entrance to the emergency department. Maya followed a few paces behind, not giving the dog any indication of where to go.

Zion sniffed around the doorway, then sat again, turning to look up at her. "Good girl," she praised, but she kept the bunny in her pocket. "Search! Search for Emily."

Understanding her job wasn't done, Zion sniffed the ground again, then went to the corner of the building. It was the side of the building that faced the parking lot. Nose to the ground, Zion trotted along the side of the building until she reached the driveway leading to the ambulance bay. Then she sat again, staring up at Maya intently.

"Good girl," she repeated. "Search for Emily."

Zion seemed to shoot her an exasperated glance before she went back to work. The husky sniffed all around the ground but returned to the exact same spot she'd alerted on before. Maya's heart sank. This appeared to be the end of the trail.

"Good girl," she said with forced enthusiasm, and tossed the bunny into the air. As always, Zion caught it and trotted along holding the stuffed animal proudly, as if she'd won the biggest prize at the state fair.

"That's impressive," Doug said from behind her. She turned to glance at him. "Your K9 reinforced my theory. I think someone parked in the ambulance bay and convinced Emily to come down along the side of the building to help. Then they kidnapped her."

She didn't like hearing that. "No video for the ambulance area?"

"No." He glanced around the area. "Can your dog track people taken away in cars?"

"No. Sometimes in the summer if the windows are open, some dogs can catch the scent if it's a calm day, but those instances are rare. It would help if we knew the general direction they were headed. We could perform a search grid."

"I've been thinking about that," Doug said thoughtfully. "Maybe we should check the closest hotels in the area, see if your K9 can pick up Emily's scent."

She frowned. "I'm not sure going from one hotel to the next is a good use of time."

"I'm open to other ideas." Doug's jaw tightened with repressed anger. "But we don't have anything else to go on. I've tried calling Emily at least twelve times. The call goes straight to voice mail. Either the phone battery died or the device is powered down."

With a grimace, she shrugged. "Okay, we'll check the hotels. But understand this, I will need to give Zion plenty of rest breaks, especially if we're outside in the cold for any length of time."

He nodded. "Of course. I wouldn't want anything to happen to your dog. If you don't mind, we can start at my hotel, the Lumberjack Inn. Emily was never there that I'm aware of. Besides, I need to let the front desk know that I'm staying longer than planned."

"That's fine." She focused on Zion. "Hand."

Zion trotted over and placed the stuffed bunny in her outstretched hand.

"She's really amazing," Doug said as they walked back to the SUV.

"Zion is one of our primary search dogs," Maya admitted. Once they were settled in the car, she drove out of the parking lot and turned west toward the Lumberjack Inn. "They're all good, but several of my sibling's K9 partners have different areas of expertise."

He nodded but didn't ask for additional information, the way most people did. His expression was grim, and she understood he was preoccupied with Emily's disappearance. She didn't like knowing the cheerful nurse who'd become a good friend to Kendra was missing. The city of Cody wasn't immune to crime, but kidnapping was rather unusual. She silently prayed that this was nothing more than a misunderstanding. That Emily knew the person who'd asked for help and would be calling Doug soon.

The moment she parked in the center of the open lot, Doug pushed his door open. "I'll get things squared away inside while you and Zion work, okay?"

"Sure." She climbed out of her seat and opened the back hatch. Zion jumped down. After closing the back, she and Zion headed toward the front entrance a few paces behind Doug.

A crack of gunfire rang out. She reacted instinctively, ducking and curling her body over her K9 as Doug whirled and plastered himself against the side of the hotel, pulling his own weapon. She darted over to the building, too, drawing Zion with her.

As they huddled against the side of the hotel, Maya couldn't help but wonder if the gunfire was related to Doug and Emily.

Or if her past had come back to haunt her?

2

Doug pressed his back against the side of the hotel. He had pulled his weapon, but the thick gloves on his hands hindered his movements, so he yanked the right glove off with his teeth so he could return fire.

First, he had to find the shooter.

He spared a quick glance toward Maya and Zion, who thankfully appeared unhurt. Relieved they were out of the line of fire, Doug edged closer to the front of the hotel, scanning the general area where the shots had come from.

Where was the gunman? With his back still pressed against the wall, he scanned the area across the street from the hotel. There were a couple of buildings, including a tavern called the Crooked Wheel, but not much else. The shooter had to be hiding over there, waiting for the opportunity to try again.

He didn't see anything for almost a full minute. Then he caught a glimpse of a man darting out from behind the Crooked Wheel and running toward a black pickup truck. Doug lunged forward, intending to catch up to them, but it was too late. The truck sped off, and he had only a second to realize the rear license plate was covered with mud. He made a note of the black older model Chevy Silverado. Hopefully, the Cody police would find the truck with the muddy plates sooner than later.

Belatedly realizing the fingers on his right hand were numb with cold, he turned to jog back to the side of the hotel. He holstered his weapon, grabbed his fallen glove, and stuffed his reddened fingers inside. Hearing the wailing sirens, he tucked his right hand beneath his armpit to warm it up as he waited for the cops to arrive.

Maybe this time they wouldn't be so quick to brush off his concerns over Emily's disappearance as it was obvious the two incidents were related.

When the Cody police squad pulled up in front of the hotel, Maya and Zion stepped forward to join him. He frowned, having expected her to leave without looking back. It was one thing to search for Emily, but being targeted by gunfire had not been part of their arrangement.

"The shooter took off in a pickup truck with muddied plates," he said. "No reason for you to be out here in the cold."

Maya arched a brow as if to indicate she'd do as she wanted. He estimated she was a few years younger than his thirty-seven, and she was beautiful with her dark hair and dark eyes. He'd been very impressed with how well she handled her husky, Zion, but the last thing he wanted was to put another woman in danger.

Having Emily gone was bad enough.

"What's this about a report of gunfire?" Officer Jones asked as he approached. The same officer who had recommended Doug seek help from those living on the Sullivan K9 Search and Rescue ranch.

"I called it in, Burt," Maya said, stepping forward. Zion stayed right at her side, blue eyes seeming to understand everything that was being said. "We were heading into the hotel when gunfire rang out. It's a miracle neither of us was hit."

Her comment gave him pause. It was strange that the shooter had missed. Most of the men and even some of the women in this part of the state were avid hunters and could hit what they were aiming at. *Maybe not as much with a handgun, though*, he silently acknowledged. Very different from shooting a rifle with the aid of a scope. He looked at Officer Jones and his senior partner, Sergeant Howell. "Obviously, this is related in some way to my sister's disappearance."

"Oh yeah? How?" Jones asked.

He bit back the flash of annoyance. These guys were treating him as if he were the bad guy in this mess. "I'm not sure, but the shooter escaped in a black older model Chevy Silverado. Maybe a 2015 or 16? I'm not sure, but the rear plate was covered in mud, so one of your patrol units should be able to find it."

The two cops exchanged a frown. "I'll call it in," Sergeant Howell said, turning away to speak into his radio.

"You seem to know a lot about cars," Jones said.

"I'm with the DEA. It's my job to be observant, including identifying vehicles used in committing crimes." He managed to keep his tone even, but it wasn't easy. Granted, he was the outsider here in Wyoming, but he suspected his being a federal agent was the real source of the officer's animosity.

"I've issued the BOLO," Sergeant Howell said. "Anything else you can remember about the perp?"

He tried to picture the guy in his mind. It happened so fast, and he had been more concerned with identifying the vehicle. "Average height and weight. That's all I can say about him."

"He wore black jeans and a black jacket," Maya added. "He wasn't wearing a cowboy hat but had one of those heavy-duty caps with flaps covering his ears."

He glanced at her in surprise. She'd caught more details than he had. "Good eye," he said. Then he brushed past the officers.

"Hey, where are you going?" Howell asked.

"Across the street." He increased his pace to reach the Crooked Wheel pub. Then he took his time examining the ground around the corner of the building where the shooter had been standing prior to darting toward the truck. It was easy to see several footprints, but like those outside the hospital, they were crisscrossed so that none were clear enough to estimate size or make of the shoe. That wasn't great, but what he really wanted to find was the shell casing.

Unfortunately, he didn't see one. Either the shooter had picked up his brass or it had fallen someplace deep into the snow.

Once again, Maya and her K9 partner joined them outside the bar. "Zion, find gold," Maya said.

Gold? Was that another way to describe brass? To his surprise, the beautiful husky lowered her nose to the ground and began sniffing the area where the shooter had been standing. It didn't take more than a minute for the husky to bury her nose in the snow. Then she pawed at the ground. When she was satisfied, she sat and looked expectantly up at Maya.

"Good girl," Maya praised. But she didn't offer the bunny until she bent over to see what the dog had found. With her gloved hand, she picked up a brass casing. "Here you go."

"Wow, that's amazing." He opened his pocket. "Drop it in, would you? Thanks."

She did, then turned her attention to her dog. "Good girl," Maya repeated with enthusiasm, this time pulling the bunny from her pocket and tossing it into the air. As before, Zion leaped up to grab it, then trotted around the area with the stuffed animal in her mouth.

"Gold, huh?" He arched a brow. "Easier for a dog to follow than brass?"

"Gold is used for gunpowder," Maya corrected. "Technically, for all sources of gunpowder and gun oil. If we're at the airport or in other public places, it's better to use a word that doesn't incite panic. We don't want the public to know we're searching for weapons."

His experience with K9s was mostly related to drug-sniffing dogs that worked the airport and main port of Lake Michigan. They used the word candy to describe drugs for a similar reason. He'd also spent some time with Matt Callahan and his K9 Duchess who had followed the trail of Brady Finnegan's young son who'd been kidnapped. A dog that could find both guns and people was interesting, and his admiration for Maya and Zion grew as he nodded. "That makes sense."

"You really think Emily's disappearance is related to this shooting?" Maya asked.

"Yeah, I do." His sister being taken from work mere hours before he was targeted by gunfire was not a coincidence. He didn't much believe in them anyway. His thoughts whirled as the situation morphed into something far more dangerous.

He needed to contact his boss to find out if any of the drug traffickers he'd put away over the past five years had recently been let out of prison. One of them must have been angry enough to track him all the way here to Wyoming.

"We'll help in any way we can," Maya said.

"No thanks. I don't want to drag you and Zion into danger." She frowned at that but didn't answer as the two Cody police officers joined them.

Doug hesitated, quickly deciding it was better to give the shell casing to the feds rather than the local cops. "Zion found a shell casing, and I'm going to get this to the feds to be put through our system. I know everyone shares the same ballistics database, but if this shooter has ties to Milwaukee, that means the criminals have crossed several state lines, putting this incident squarely within federal jurisdiction."

"You do know the local police and the feds share the same state crime lab in Cheyenne, right?" Sergeant Howell drawled.

"Really?" He glanced at Maya who nodded.

"Tom is right. Local labs can do basics, but anything forensic goes to the state lab," she confirmed.

He inwardly groaned. Knowing Cheyenne was on the opposite side of the state, he felt certain driving there was his only option.

"It would be nice if you'd keep us in the loop," Jones said after a moment of silence. "Emily is one of ours, and we'd like to know when she's found."

When, not if. He liked that the cops were thinking positive. He tried to do the same. "I will." Yet despite his determination to keep his hopes up, he realized the responsibility of finding his sister rested squarely on his shoulders.

And failure was not an option.

DESPITE HER BEST efforts to remain neutral, Maya found herself intrigued by DEA Agent Doug Bridges. It wasn't that he was handsome—she'd been divorced for five years and had no interest in heading down that path again. But his intense concern about his half sister, combined with his nonchalant attitude toward being shot at, was an enigma.

She was tempted to mention her concerns about being followed, then decided against it. Doug was probably right. The gunfire so close on the heels of Emily's disappearance indicated a likely connection.

This wasn't about her. Yet that didn't mean she was about to cut and run either.

"Every search I perform with Zion carries a level of risk," she said, getting back to his comment. "And I hate to say this, but I doubt you'll find Emily without our help."

He scowled. "I agree that you would be a huge asset in finding Emily, but I don't want you or Zion to get hurt."

"I don't want that either," she said. Dipping her gloved hand into her coat pocket, she pulled out her handgun. "Like just about every Wyoming resident, I have a carry concealed permit. I can also hit what I'm aiming for. You should know that I once worked in law enforcement, not here, but in Cheyenne. I was a K9 cop there." She tried not to show her true feelings about her time as an officer. First, she'd lost her K9 partner Ranger in a shooting gone wrong. Then her ex-husband, Blaine, had made it clear her job was the reason their marriage had fallen apart. As if it was her fault he'd cheated on her. The jerk. Right after they'd separated, she'd gotten the devastating news her parents had died, forcing her back to living on the ranch. Despite the horrible losses, moving home had been the best decision. She'd taken their mission of performing search and rescue work to heart and wasn't about to stop now. "Look, let's get back to work. Arguing won't get the job done. Besides, it's cold out here."

Doug had looked surprised to see the gun, and he finally nodded. "Okay, you're right. I could use your help. And I'm freezing. Let's get back to the Lumberjack Inn to warm up. I still need to extend my stay."

She held out her hand to Zion who dutifully dropped the bunny into it. Tucking the toy into her left pocket, the one that didn't contain the gun, she gave Zion the hand signal to heel and followed Doug back across the street to the hotel.

The interior of the hotel was blessedly warm, and she gravitated toward the beautiful stone fireplace located directly across from the front desk, grateful to absorb the heat from the flames. Zion lifted her nose, sniffing with curiosity. Maya had come to understand that even without issuing search or find commands, her partner often knew her role was to keep searching for those who were missing.

Like Emily.

As she waited for Doug to chat with the desk clerk, she wondered if she should call Kendra to let her youngest sibling know about Emily. Then she decided against it. Kendra and her K9, Smoky, would want to participate in the search, even though she was barely healed from her fall. Considering the recent bout of gunfire, Maya wasn't willing to put the baby of the family in danger.

They'd lost their parents five years ago after a horrible plane crash in the mountains. As the eldest, Maya and Chase had worked hard to keep the family together. Ironically, their parents had been wealthy in a way that none of them had fully realized. It had been Maya's idea to turn the ranch into a K9 search and rescue business. Their reputation had flourished, reaching across several states. They didn't take money for the jobs they accepted. The only payments that were welcome were bags of dog food. Mostly because there were nine dogs on the ranch, and keeping them fed was a monumental task.

After the way they'd lost their parents, she and Chase had been a bit overprotective of Kendra. She'd taken the loss of their parents hard and kept insisting their parents' death wasn't an accident.

Privately, she and Chase had agreed. And they had tried to do their own investigation without much success.

No, she wouldn't drag Kendra into this now. One Sullivan in danger was more than enough. She would not call on the rest of her siblings for help unless necessary.

The way things were going, she sensed her role in the search would be rather limited. She wasn't convinced that searching the local hotels for Emily's scent was the right way to proceed. They'd need something more tangible to go on.

What, she wasn't sure.

She glanced over her shoulder to see that Doug was no longer standing at the front desk. The clerk sensed her gaze, then quickly looked away, pretending to be busy with her computer. Maya frowned, wondering what was going on.

Five minutes later, she had her answer. Doug strolled toward her dragging his computer and laptop case. "Looks like I'll need a new place to stay," he said in response to her surprised look.

"What happened? The hotel can't possibly be booked solid this time of the year."

"I was told in no uncertain terms that I needed to find somewhere else to stay." He shrugged. "Guess being targeted by gunfire and having cops show up is cause for alarm."

A flash of anger hit hard. Zion sensed her turbulent

emotions and moved closer to her side. "That's ridiculous. They can't force you to leave."

"It doesn't matter." Doug didn't look overly concerned. "I'll find somewhere else to stay." He offered a lopsided grin. "That can be our excuse to have Zion sniffing around other local hotels."

It was tempting to offer him her guest room at the Sullivan K9 Search and Rescue ranch, but she managed to swallow the urge. She didn't really know anything about Doug Bridges, other than his half sister Emily was missing and someone had tried to kill him. But even if he was harmless, there was an unwritten rule against offering those who needed their services a place to stay. The ranch was remote, and she didn't want to be stuck with an unwanted guest.

Besides, getting emotionally involved wasn't smart. The best way to find a missing person was to stay detached from emotional entanglements. She had no intention of crossing that line now.

"I'll have Zion search for Emily here," she said. "Then we'll hit the road." She eyed him curiously. "Sounds like you want to head all the way to Cheyenne to drop off the evidence."

Doug nodded. "Yeah, I do. Thanks for staying a bit. My car is still at the veterinary office building. No reason for you to worry about driving across the state. I can do that myself."

She opened the bag containing Emily's gloves and offered it to Zion. "Search for Emily."

Zion sniffed the bag for barely two seconds before turning to sniff along the floor of the lobby. Maya knew Zion was smart enough to know Emily's scent without being reminded. Her K9 went all the way through the area without alerting.

Not a surprise. Maya would have been shocked if Emily

had been in the hotel, especially if she hadn't been there to visit Doug.

She pushed open the doors, wincing at the cold blast of air that greeted them. Zion eagerly trotted outside, not noticing the cold with her thick coat. Her dog sniffed all along the sidewalk, then took a zigzag pattern across the parking lot. Still no alert.

"Come, Zion," she called. She imagined the K9 was disappointed the search game was over as she trotted back toward her. She glanced at Doug. "Sorry, but as you can see, there's no indication Emily has been here."

"Thanks for trying." His expression didn't reveal his disappointment. Or maybe he was just that good at hiding his emotions.

They returned to her K9-adapted SUV. She opened the back hatch for Zion, then gestured to the back seat. "Put your suitcase and laptop there, okay?"

He nodded and opened the back passenger seat to store his things. Moments later, they were situated in the front seat with the heat blasting from the vents.

"How long will it take to get to the lab in Cheyenne?" Doug asked. "I took a moment to check out our options, seems that Wyoming doesn't have an actual field office like ours in Milwaukee."

"At least five and a half hours, maybe more depending on how well the roads have been cleared." She glanced at him. "The other option is to charter a plane."

He winced. "Twelve hours round trip? I can't even imagine being that far from the crime lab."

"Yep, that's how it is out here." She felt bad for him; people who came to Wyoming didn't realize how large the state was. And how far away the main cities were from each other. "In my opinion, we should do some work with Zion first, even though searching the various hotels is pretty much a long shot. After that, you can decide whether you'd rather drive or fly."

"Yeah, okay." He poked at his phone screen. "There aren't too many hotels in the area anyway. I have a list here on my phone."

She hid a smile. "No need to look them up, I know where they are." She pulled out from the parking lot of the Lumberjack Inn and drove to the next hotel located barely a half mile down the road. "I've lived in this area for my entire life. I know my way around. The Elk Lodge is the nicest of the bunch."

"It may be too close," he muttered. "Do you think these hotel clerks talk to each other? I might be blacklisted from most of them."

She shrugged. "Only one way to find out."

After letting Zion out of the back, she told the dog to search for Emily's scent. Her K9 was anxious to please, but after several long minutes, it was clear Emily hadn't been there.

Doug came outside, shaking his head in disgust. "No rooms available at this time," he said. "Can you believe that?"

Actually, she couldn't. It wasn't normal for hotels to turn down paying customers during the long winter months. "I'm sorry," she said. "I'm sure we'll have better luck on the other side of town."

Unfortunately, that wasn't the case. By the time they'd reached the third hotel, Maya had to admit the news of a shooting involving a federal agent had spread across the town faster than wildfire.

"I guess I'll sleep on the sofa at Emily's place," Doug said with a sigh as they climbed back into the SUV. "She gave me the code to get inside her garage. I was using the hotel in the first place because she only has a two-bedroom home, and the spare room had been turned into an office."

"That's probably best," Maya agreed, squashing a flash of guilt over his situation. "I feel bad about this. Usually we're nicer to strangers."

He waved that off. "There's only one more place to check, the Wild Bill Motel. Gotta say, it looks rather worn down."

"It's not a top-tier establishment, that's for sure," she said with a wry nod. "I didn't work in Cody as a cop, but I did find a missing girl here once. Turned out she had left Jackson to work here as a prostitute. With the help of the Cody police, we broke up the prostitution ring."

Doug frowned. "Sounds like exactly the type of place a criminal might bring a missing woman."

She shrugged, eyeing Zion in the rearview mirror. Despite going out into the cold weather, her partner was still raring to go. "If he was stupid enough to stay in town, yes. But there are plenty of places to hide outside of the city limits. You'd be surprised at how many abandoned cabins and hunting shacks are in the area. Granted, January is our coldest month of the year, so they'd need one with a wood stove or risk freezing to death."

"Great." He scowled. "We'll never find her at this rate."

"We're doing everything possible," she said, trying to sound encouraging. But his keen despair radiated off him in waves.

Doug grimaced when he got his first look at the Wild Bill Motel. Seeing it through his eyes, she could see why. The place had fallen into disrepair over the past several years. The roof shingles were beginning to curl, the walls needed at least three coats of paint, and she knew from experience the interior rooms were old, shabby, and musty. No surprise it was still known to be a place where rooms could be rented by the hour.

The local cops probably visited the place on a regular basis. Maybe Doug had a point about this location being a perfect place to hide Emily.

She let Zion out of the back. Zion stared up at her, anticipating the command. She bypassed the routine of offering water and the scent source to speed things along. Holding the dog's gaze, she said, "Search for Emily."

Zion went to work, first testing the air with her nose, then lowering her head to sniff along the row of parking spaces positioned in front of each motel room door. Maya decided to enter the lobby last. If Zion didn't find Emily outside any of the rooms, alerting on her scent inside the lobby wouldn't mean much. Emily could have been inside simply to meet with someone.

Zion made it all the way to room six of ten when she abruptly stopped and sniffed all along the base of the doorway. Maya's heart thudded in her chest when Zion sat and stared up at her.

"Is she alerting on Emily's scent?" Doug asked.

"It appears so." She barely got the words out, when Doug rushed forward and pounded his fist on the door. Startled by his frantic approach, Zion let out a sharp bark and backed away. Not a smart move on his part. Maya gave Zion the hand signal for come, and the dog quickly returned to her side.

She wasn't sure if she should reward her K9 partner or not. Was Emily really inside the room?

"Federal agent!" Doug shouted between thundering knocks. "Open the door and come out with your hands up!"

There was no movement from within the room from

what she could see. Doug tried again, then turned and ran into the lobby. Before she could blink, he emerged holding a key card in his hand.

Apparently, being a fed had its perks. She could just imagine the scared clerk caving to his order to hand over the master key. It didn't take long to access the room. Maya pulled her weapon from her pocket, taking a step forward to protect Zion as she waited to see what happened.

As the seconds ticked by into a full two minutes, she realized the room must have been empty. Doug poked his head out from the doorway, his expression crestfallen. "Maya? Can you ask Zion to check the room?"

"Of course." She tucked her weapon back into her pocket and walked over to meet him. Zion kept pace at her side. Pausing at the threshold, she looked down at her K9. "Search for Emily."

Zion lowered her nose and entered the room. She took her time; there were probably hundreds of thousands of scents to sift through. Then she alerted near the side of the bed, staring up at Maya with her intense gaze. She managed to respond, "Good girl," and tossed the stuffed bunny in her direction.

Then she glanced at Doug. Her heart squeezed as his green eyes filled with anguish. Emily had been there, likely recently. Yet that wasn't good enough.

They needed more.

They needed to know where Emily was being held captive. Before it was too late.

3

Doug hated knowing Emily had been brought to this sleazebag motel but tried not to dwell on the reason why she'd been taken. He needed answers, and that idiot pimple-faced clerk was going to give them to him.

"Let's go to the lobby," he said. "I need to know who rented this room."

Maya searched his gaze for a moment, then nodded and stepped back into the cold. "Come, Zion."

He understood what she hadn't said. That most of these rooms were given out for cash, therefore making it impossible to track those involved in criminal activity. But he had no intention of leaving without answers. He wasn't a violent man by nature, but he would not hesitate to bring the full force of the federal government down upon this place if they didn't cooperate.

Lengthening his stride, he pulled the lobby door open, letting Maya and Zion go in first. Following on their heels, he brushed past them to confront the clerk. "Here's your key." He slapped it on the counter. "I want to know who was in room six over the past twenty-four hours."

"I can't tell you that." The kid quickly took the key as if anxious to hide the fact that he'd given it out in the first place.

Doug pulled out his badge again and held it up at the pimply kid's eye level. "Do you really want me to get a federal search warrant to tear this place apart? We'll shut it down for however long it takes to ensure no drug or human trafficking has taken place here." When the kid blanched, he added, "Could be one week. Two. Maybe longer. Trust me, I'll take my sweet time."

"I-I want to cooperate, really. But I don't know!" The kid visibly shrank back from him. "He paid in cash."

Knowing the perp was male was a start. "Did you recognize him? Is he a local?"

"I—no, I didn't recognize him." The kid's gaze darted to Maya, as if hoping she might intervene on his behalf. When help wasn't forthcoming, he looked back at Doug. "I don't think he was a local; he had a funny accent."

"Funny how?" Doug demanded, doing his best not to reach across the counter to shake the truth out of him. "Like mine? From the Midwest? Or maybe a drawl like from the South?"

"Maybe the South." The kid did not sound the least bit convincing.

Doug strove for patience. "Okay, what did he look like? Tall, short, fat, or thin? What race is he? Did you see what car he was driving? I need details. I want you to tell me everything about this guy you can remember."

"I don't know." The clerk's tone was whiny.

He narrowed his gaze and slapped his palms on the countertop. "Think! I need answers."

The clerk took a hasty step back. "Okay, yeah, I uh, think he had brown skin and dark hair. He didn't tell me his name, and I didn't ask."

"What else?" he pressed.

The whiny tone returned. "I don't know. He was average. Not fat or thin. Not super tall either. I didn't see his truck."

"If you didn't see it, how did you know he drove a truck?" Doug demanded.

"I, uh . . ." Again, he glanced toward Maya as if seeking help. "I think he had a pickup truck. It was near the front door. I didn't really pay any attention."

"Were there other people in the truck?" He thought about the Silverado that took off from the scene of the shooting.

The clerk scrunched his face. "I, yeah, I think so."

Doug curled his fingers into fists.

The kid noticed, flinched, then said, "I didn't pay attention! My job is to rent rooms while minding my own business. I'm not supposed to ask questions, you know? I'm just supposed to bring in money."

Doug leaned forward, his gaze fierce. "Speaking of that money, how much goes into your pocket rather than being funneled to the owner?"

The clerk's jaw dropped in shock, but he managed to recover. "None! I swear."

Doug didn't believe him. He briefly considered bribing him for more information on the brown-skinned guy who'd been in the room. Yet at the same time, he didn't trust the kid not to provide false intel just to get the cash. He leaned even closer, getting into the kid's face. "If I find out you lied to me, I'll be back. And it won't be with a search warrant. I'll take care of you—personally."

The implied threat had the kid swallowing hard. "I'm

not lying about the brown-skinned dude. Not from the rez, but maybe Hispanic? He asked for a room for two nights. We don't often get extended stays. I gave it to him. That's all I know."

Two nights? That gave him pause. He'd assumed that grabbing Emily had been a crime of opportunity. An impulse to take a pretty girl. But two days made it sound as if the crime may have been premeditated.

Because of him? His stomach twisted painfully. Was the Hispanic perp someone he'd once arrested and tossed in jail for drug trafficking? Doug hadn't anticipated that anyone would have made the connection between him and his half sister, Emily Sanders.

But their relationship wasn't exactly a secret either. Anyone who was technically savvy could find birth, marriage, and divorce records. His parents had split twenty-seven years ago, when he was ten years old. His mother had moved away from Wisconsin to marry her old high school sweetheart, Tim Sanders, who lived and worked in the natural gas industry in Wyoming. They had Emily a year later. Now Emily was twenty-six and had been taken someplace against her will.

He had to force himself to turn away from the trembling clerk. He should feel bad for his threatening actions, but he didn't. The trail was already growing cold. He desperately needed to find Emily before they . . .

No. Don't. He took a deep breath, refusing to finish his dark thought.

"Would you like a ride back to Emily's house?" Maya asked.

"Not yet." He abruptly turned back to the clerk. "That room stays empty until I can get a crime team out here to check for fingerprints and DNA. Understand?" He lifted his hand, wiggling his fingers. "I need that key back. Now."

"Sure." The kid hastily retrieved the key and returned it to the counter. "Whatever you say."

Taking it, Doug was forced to admit he'd gotten as much information as possible from the clerk. Which wasn't much. And since the motel rented rooms by the hour, he didn't have high hopes of finding prints or DNA that would lead to Emily's kidnapper.

But he had to try.

"I need to call the Cody police again," he said, pulling his phone from his pocket. "I can't leave until their crime scene techs arrive."

"You don't want federal crime scene techs to process the room?" Maya asked in surprise. "You didn't give the locals your shell casing."

"I know, but I should have. I didn't realize the lab was so far away. And now we need this evidence collected too." The charm of being near the Bighorn Mountains was wearing thin. He was beginning to resent the fact that Wyoming was such a spread-out state, with their largest cities hours apart. "Once they gather the evidence, and we get it to the state crime lab, we can fast-track it through federal channels. That's the best I can do."

"Makes sense," she agreed. She bent to scratch Zion behind the ears. "Lie down," she said. The dog obediently lowered her frame to the floor, resting her head between her front paws.

A stab of guilt hit hard. What right did he have to tie up a valuable resource like this? Zion had done her job; he didn't really need Maya and her husky to wait around for the crime scene techs. "There's no reason for you and Zion to stick around. I appreciate everything you've done for me and Emily, but I feel bad taking up your time. Especially since you haven't even let me pay for your services."

"It's okay." Maya shrugged. "We don't have anything pressing to do."

A wave of relief hit hard, mostly because he felt a bit like a stranger dropped into an alien land. "Thank you. And please know I don't mind paying your going rate. Whatever it takes. I just need to find Emily."

"I want to find Emily too," Maya said softly. "And if you insist on paying, I'll take a bag of dog food."

"A bag of dog food?" He wasn't sure he'd heard correctly.

"Yep. That's the going rate. Dog food." She smiled. "You have no idea how much food nine K9s go through in a week."

Nine dogs? He had no idea there were that many K9s on the ranch. He shrugged and nodded. "Done. I'll get that to you by the end of the day." He turned away to make his call to the Cody police. He reached a different officer this time, one who didn't sound enthusiastic about sending a crime scene team to the Wild Bill Motel until Doug mentioned his missing sister and his role within the federal government. And meeting the two officers earlier after there was gunfire outside his hotel.

"That was you? I heard about that call. Okay, I'll send Cindy and Bart over ASAP," Officer Johnson said.

Two people? He swallowed a groan. Wyoming had lots of mountains and big open spaces. But the personnel side of things was sorely lacking.

Lowering his phone, he caught Maya's empathetic gaze. "I've worked a couple of cases with Cindy and Bart," she said. "They're very good."

He appreciated her attempt to make him feel better. "Thanks. I'm just used to . . . bigger teams."

"We manage to get the job done," she said lightly. "Having more people doesn't always equate to better outcomes."

The local police had raved about the Sullivans' K9 success rate, so he nodded without saying anything more.

He had never been much for praying, although he'd recently experienced that sort of thing firsthand with the Callahans, Finnegans, and Rhy's tactical team. But maybe he should.

He stared out at the cloudy sky, silently asking God to keep Emily safe. For her sake, if not for his.

MAYA HAD BEEN surprised Doug had managed to get any information from Lewis Pally, the Wild Bill desk clerk. She remembered him from when she found the missing girl. He had not been cooperative then either. Maybe Doug's federal badge had scared him.

Or his intimidating attitude. Watching Doug in action had been impressive.

Not that they'd learned much. Knowing their perp was Hispanic was helpful, but not to the point he would be easy to find. Many Hispanics worked on ranches in the area.

And she was convinced they were looking for at least two perps, maybe more. She believed Lewis had seen a second person in the truck. In her humble opinion, it would have taken at least two men to hold Emily against her will.

It didn't make sense, though, that they'd brought Emily to the Wild Bill only to turn around and leave. Doug's idea of checking motels had paid off, but she didn't understand exactly what they were dealing with.

Sex trafficking? If so, leaving the motel so soon didn't

follow. If Emily had been taken to work as a prostitute, she'd still be here. Unless they had another place to hold the girls?

Back when she was a cop in Cheyenne, the girls snagged clients from the local tavern and used the closest motel as their workplace. Unfortunately, there were plenty of down-on-their-luck women who chose that way to make money. She hadn't encountered any women who'd been forced into having sex for money.

But it had been several years, and maybe things had changed for the worst. She could tell Doug was struggling not to dwell the ramifications of Emily's kidnapping.

"There they are," Doug said, breaking into her thoughts.

She nodded, seeing the white van pulling into the parking lot.

"Wait here," he said. "No sense in both of us freezing to death."

She hid a smile as he strode out to greet the crime scene techs. When her phone rang, she frowned when she saw her brother Chase was calling. "Hey, what's up?"

"You tell me." His tone was curt. "I got a call from Angela, Dr. Andrew's vet tech. She was concerned you rescheduled at the last minute when you were right outside the building. What's going on?"

This was the curse of living near a small town. Their family ranch was located forty miles southeast of Cody, but news still traveled fast. "I'm fine. A federal agent asked for my help to find his sister. You remember when Kendra fell? Her nurse, Emily, has gone missing."

"Federal agent?" Trust her brother to zero in on the least important part of the conversation. Even though he was one year her junior, Chase was protective over his sisters. Probably an ethereal directive from their late father. "From Cheyenne?"

"No, he's here visiting from Wisconsin. His name is Doug Bridges, and he's Emily's half brother." She tried not to sigh and decided not to mention the shooting incident targeting Doug. "I'm fine, Chase. And so is Zion. I'm still in Cody as Zion was able to track Emily's scent to the Wild Bill Motel."

"That's not good," Chase muttered. "Talk about a hot bed of crime."

"Yeah, well, she's not here now." She glanced at her watch, somewhat surprised to note it was only ten in the morning. Oddly, it seemed later. "I'm not sure when I'll get back to the ranch. Let the rest of the sibs know I'm on a case."

"Yeah, okay. Anna will be upset if you're not back for dinner, though," Chase said, mentioning their housekeeper. It wasn't so much that they couldn't take care of themselves, but more that they were often called out on various calls especially during the peak tourist season. Anna helped keep the ranch running smoothly. "You know how she worries."

"I'll let her know if I'm not going to make it home," she promised. Seeing Doug heading toward the lobby, she added, "I have to go. Later."

"Later," her brother said, before she ended the call.

Doug's somber expression made her stomach clench. "What's wrong?"

He stood for a moment, as if soaking in the warmth. "Looks like the room was pretty much wiped clean. And get this, the bed linens and a few of the towels were taken too. Your techs, Cindy and Bart, are going to look in some of the more remote places, like inside drawers and the toilet paper roll, that sort of thing." He blew out a breath. "They may find something, useful, but it's not looking good."

"That's odd. It's not a common practice for small-time

criminals to take the time to wipe down a motel room," she said thoughtfully. "And for sure they wouldn't steal bed linens."

"I wondered about that." He scrubbed his chin. "It makes me think these guys were smart enough not to leave any DNA evidence behind. I still have the shell casing. Maybe I should drive to Cheyenne. If nothing else, I wouldn't mind talking to the federal agent there myself."

"Do you want me to drive you there? I'm familiar with the area." She couldn't blame him for wanting to talk to his colleague here in Wyoming. Getting the shell casing fast-tracked was their best option for getting information.

"No need, I can drive myself." He crossed over to toss the key card on the counter. Lewis Pally was doing his best to pretend to be working, avoiding Doug's gaze. When Doug slapped his hand on the counter, Lewis startled badly. "What?"

"This is my business card," Doug said, pushing it across the counter. "I need you to call me if you see the brown-skinned Hispanic man again. Or the truck. Understand?"

"Uh, yeah. Sure." When Lewis didn't immediately take the card, Doug scowled and took a menacing step forward. That was enough to force Lewis to hastily grab it. "Okay. Okay, I'll call," he said.

"You better. Don't make me follow through on my threat." With that, Doug turned back toward her. "Let's get out of here."

"Come, Zion," she said. Her partner jumped up, stretched, then trotted alongside her as they went back out to her SUV. She hit the button to open the back hatch. Zion didn't hesitate to gracefully leap in.

As they waited for the engine to warm up, Doug said,

"Before we go to pick up my SUV, I need to stop by Emily's house again."

She shot him a curious look. When he didn't expound on his reasoning, she shrugged. "Okay, I'm not sure where she lives, though. My sister Kendra has been there, but I haven't."

"She's not far from the hospital, which isn't far from the veterinary office." He paused, then asked, "Your sister Kendra knew Emily?"

She forgot she hadn't given him any information about the family. "I'm the oldest of nine siblings." She pulled out of the motel parking lot. "Kendra is the youngest and fell down a ravine during a search and rescue operation last month. She spent several hours in the emergency department, and your sister, Emily, was her nurse." She drove back toward the hospital. "They became close during that time, probably because they're close in age. Emily was new to the area, and Kendra wanted to make her feel welcome here."

"Nine?" He gaped in shock. "I know one other family that has nine kids; their last name is Finnegan. What are the odds that I'd run into another large family on the other side of the country?"

"I have no idea." She glanced over at him. "Our family is pretty much an anomaly out here."

"I can imagine." He looked thoughtful for a moment. "It's probably a fool's errand going back to Emily's place, but I was struck by the fact that the brown-skinned possibly Hispanic perp rented the room for a few days. Makes me think he targeted my sister on purpose rather than just coming across her outside the hospital and acting on impulse."

"I had the same concern," she agreed. "But why does that require a ride back to Emily's house?"

"I should have thought of this earlier, but I installed a camera doorbell as a Christmas gift. Emily thought I was crazy, as there isn't much crime out here, but she lives alone, so I insisted. I'd like to review the video, see if I can catch a glimpse of a truck or car passing by." He frowned. "I don't have her doorbell software connected to my phone or laptop since I don't live in the area. But I can bring it up on her computer. She gave me her password so I could set everything up."

"Great idea." She didn't have a lot of experience with that level of security. Nine overly protective dogs were far more effective than cameras in keeping intruders at bay. Especially since having a nine-hundred-acre ranch meant they didn't have any neighbors.

"It's driving me crazy that we don't have anything more to go on," Doug said. "Up ahead, take a left turn at the intersection. Emily's house is a half mile down the road."

"I hope you were joking about beating Lewis to a pulp," she said as she made the turn. "He's a scumbag, but assault is still against the law."

"I was joking. Mostly." He grimaced. "I have never taken my anger out on a perp or a reluctant witness. But I can't deny he made me angry. It was like pulling teeth to get him to talk."

"Yeah, I know." She decided her initial instinct regarding Doug being a decent guy was on track. Not that she had been concerned about him physically attacking her. His angst over his missing sister and the fact that he was targeted by gunfire were key indicators that Emily was in danger. "Do you think this is related to one of your DEA cases back home?"

"I don't know, but it's a possibility we can't ignore." He

gestured with his hand. "That's Emily's place, the third one down."

She identified the small home and pulled into the driveway. "Do you want us to wait out here?"

He hesitated, then shook his head. "You better come inside where it's warm. I don't know how long this will take."

"Okay." Giving Zion more time with Emily's scent couldn't hurt. Zion was good, but every so often her partner became distracted by other new and interesting scents. Huskies had a high play drive, which made them good search dogs. Keeping them active, though, could be a challenge. She hit the button to open the back door, then pushed out to join her K9.

She told Zion to get busy—the phrase they used back at the ranch, which basically meant go to the bathroom. Zion was well trained enough to pee on command. Then she and Zion followed Doug inside Emily's house.

It was small, and she quickly found Doug in the second bedroom turned office, booting up the computer. She turned and took Zion into Emily's bedroom. She didn't like invading the young woman's privacy, but this was the best way to keep Zion focused.

Crossing to the laundry hamper, she bent over to pull up a woolen sock. "Emily," she said, offering the sock to Zion. "This is Emily."

The husky obliged by pressing her nose into the sock. Then she looked up at Maya with her pale-blue eyes as if to say, *Yes, I remember*.

"Emily," she repeated, placing the sock in the bag with the gloves. In her experience, socks were a better scent source than gloves. One of the reasons dogs loved chewing on socks and shoes is that those items held the strongest scent of their owners. "We're going to find Emily." She didn't use the search command, as it was clear the small home was empty. And Emily's scent was everywhere.

Zion wagged her tail in agreement.

She moved through the small house, then returned to the office. Doug had shrugged out of his coat and was hunched over the computer. His intense gaze was focused on the screen. He didn't even look up as she and Zion entered.

"I'm almost finished," he said, proving her assumption that he hadn't noticed her wrong. "I'm fast-forwarding through this and have yet to see the Silverado truck. Or anything thing else remotely suspicious."

"No problem." She turned to head back to the kitchen.

"Wait! Look at this!" His voice rose with excitement. "Yesterday morning shortly after Emily came home from work. See it? Is that the same black Silverado truck?"

She came around the corner of the desk to peer over his shoulder. "It could be. To be honest, I didn't see it as clearly as you did."

"Twenty-four hours ago, the black truck is going past her house. Then we see someone jump inside after firing at me." He shook his head. "I don't think that's a coincidence."

"Maybe, but it's not much of a clue either," she felt compelled to point out. "There are a lot of big trucks out here. Ranchers and residents prefer them, especially for our unpredictable wintery weather."

"Yeah I know, but still." His fingers danced along the keyboard. "I've sent the video to my email. Maybe my tech guy back home can do something with it." He pushed back from the desk. "Let's go. Before I head south, I'd like to buy you lunch. I haven't eaten since last night."

After a moment's hesitation, she nodded. There was no reason for her to go with him to Cheyenne, other than she couldn't ignore the strange urge to stick close. It wasn't logical, but finding Emily was their primary goal. Doug seemed determined to reimburse her in some way. She had no intention of mentioning how she and her siblings had inherited several million dollars after her parents were killed.

She followed Doug to the doorway, giving Zion the hand signal to come. Doug opened the door, turning to say something when another crack of gunfire rang out.

"Down!" he shouted hoarsely, ducking to the side and slamming the door shut. The shooter didn't stop at one round this time. Several bullets peppered the door.

Then there was nothing but silence.

4

What in the world was going on? Doug's heart thundered in his chest as he stared at the bullet-ridden door.

This time, the shooter had gotten far too close.

"Are you hit?" Maya asked, her voice tense.

"No, you?" He glanced over his shoulder to where Maya and Zion were huddled behind the kitchen table, the only source of protection nearby. Zion was under the table, but Maya had her weapon in hand. He was impressed that her cop instincts had kicked in. From what he could tell, they weren't hurt. But seeing three small dark bullet holes in the cabinets behind her shook him to the core.

Way too close.

"We're fine. I'll call the police." She reached for her phone.

"No, don't bother." He shook his head. "We can't stay here. I'll provide cover so we can get out of here long enough for you and Zion to head back to your ranch."

She shot him an exasperated glance and proceeded with her call. "Yes, this is Maya Sullivan reporting several rounds of gunfire at the residence of Emily Sanders, on Baker Street. Send officers to the scene ASAP."

He swallowed hard against a wave of frustration. This was ridiculous. Just because she carried a gun and once worked in law enforcement didn't mean he wanted her caught in the cross fire of whatever danger surrounded him and Emily.

Mostly him. This second attempt to shoot him sealed his belief that whoever had taken Emily had done so to get to him. He was surprised he hadn't gotten some sort of ransom call by now. These guys must want something. If the goal was to kill him, the way they seemed to be trying to do, then why take Emily in the first place?

It didn't make any sense. Yet the danger had escalated to a point where he needed to get Maya and Zion out of there.

"We need to move," he said again. "Let's go out the back. We can skirt the edge of the house and make sure the coast is clear before we make a run for the car."

"We're staying until the local police arrive," she corrected. "And from there, I'll see if Zion can find more shell casings. You need to check your camera video again to see if the shooter came by in the Silverado truck."

Her calm attitude under pressure was admirable. And since he could already hear the wail of sirens, he gave up trying to argue. She had a valid point about the video.

Moving toward the window overlooking the street, he waited until the two squads pulled up in front of the house before heading over to open the bullet-ridden front door. Two different officers headed toward him, and he wondered if the city of ten thousand residents had just four cops on duty on each shift. A level of staffing difficult to comprehend.

The officer closest to him had a name tag identifying

him as Rotterdam. He whistled when he saw the damaged door. "Who did this?"

"Probably the same shooter that fired at us from the Crooked Wheel." He stepped back to give them room to enter. "I was just going to check the security video."

"Hey, Frank, Wayne," Maya greeted the two officers. "This is federal agent Doug Bridges; his sister Emily Sanders went missing early this morning. We've identified a black Chevy Silverado as belonging to the perps, but the license plate has been covered with mud."

"Yeah, we got the BOLO on that." Doug noticed Wayne's name tag read Carter. "Did you see anything?"

Doug shook his head. "No, the bullets started flying the minute I opened the door." He turned to head back to Emily's office. He quickly logged into his sister's computer, then pulled up the recent video from outside the front door.

Maya came up behind him. He scowled when he saw what appeared to be the same black Silverado roll into view. The passenger-side window lowered revealing a man dressed in black with a ski mask covering his face. He leaned out and fired repeatedly toward the house. Then the vehicle took off, disappearing down the street.

"I guess that proves our theory," Maya said. "Looks like the same vehicle to me."

"Me too." He quickly copied the video and sent it to his personal email. He briefly considered taking the time to install Emily's doorbell camera software on his phone but decided against it.

There was no reason for these guys to return. They'd expect him to go on the run again.

It occurred to him that their goal may not necessarily be to outright kill him, but to keep him preoccupied with running for cover so he couldn't find Emily.

Although the six bullets poked a few holes in that thought. One bullet could be viewed as a distraction. Not six.

"What did you find?" Frank asked, entering the room.

Doug slammed the computer and stood. "Give me your email address, I'll send both videos to you. Unfortunately, the camera angle is such that the license plate can't be seen. Not even to confirm that it's covered in mud."

Frank and Wayne exchanged a grim look. "We'll take whatever you have."

Doug pulled up his email. After punching in Frank's email address with the Cody police department, he sent the two videos, then pocketed his phone. He was back in work mode. "I know your two crime scene techs, Cindy and Bart, are tied up at the Wild Bill Motel, so I'll retrieve the slugs." He glanced at Maya. "If you and Zion can search for the additional shell casings, that would be great. I'm still planning to head to Cheyenne with the evidence."

Again, the officers looked at each other. "Not sure why you called us," Wayne Carter drawled.

"We're counting on the Cody police to find that black Silverado truck," Maya said in a placating tone. "I know there's only four of you on duty, but we believe this truck was used to kidnap Emily Sanders. Finding it will be the best way to resolve this case."

Doug nodded, understanding they needed the cops on their side. "Please, keep an eye out for it," he said. "The only reason I'm taking the bullet fragments and shell casings to the state lab is to put a rush on the ballistics to see if they pop in the system. I can't help but think these guys are related to one of my previous cases. Likely one of the crooks I put away has come to seek revenge."

That seemed to mollify the officers. "Okay, we'll help you get those slugs."

"No need, I'd rather you both head outside to watch over Maya and Zion in case those gunmen come back." He edged past them toward the kitchen. "This won't take long."

Maya rolled her eyes at his comment but didn't argue as she shrugged into her winter coat. "Come, Zion. Are you ready? It's time to search for gold."

The K9 wagged her tail and eagerly followed Maya outside. Frank and Wayne stayed close, giving Doug plenty of room to pull a steak knife from Emily's drawer and go to work extracting bullets. Agents didn't often retrieve their own evidence, but he knew enough not to get too close to the slugs themselves. Instead, he carved a half inch around them until he had three chunks of cabinet wood on the table.

He hunted for the other three slugs. One was embedded deep in the wall; the other two were halfway across the living room. As he went to work on those, his heart flared with hope when he realized they weren't as badly mangled as the others.

"We only found two casings," Maya said, coming back inside with the brass in the palm of her hand. "I was glad to find them. The perp shot from inside the car, so I figure most of them are still inside the vehicle."

"Great." He rummaged through Emily's kitchen drawers to find plastic bags. He held it open for Maya to drop those two shell casings inside. Then he grabbed another bag for the casing still in his pocket. Better to keep them separated in case they were dealing with more than one firearm.

Then he used a larger bag for the bullet fragments. Once he had all the evidence in one large bag, he stood for a moment surveying the kitchen. He felt awful about how much damage had been done. Then he turned away, making a silent promise to reimburse Emily for the repairs. Not that she'd care.

Property damage was nothing compared to the fact that his sister was still missing.

And for the second time in a matter of hours, he found himself praying that God would keep Emily safe until he could find and rescue her.

After Maya had rewarded Zion for her find, she mentally replayed this most recent gunfire incident over and over in her mind. Had the shooter intended to take out Doug? Or had he targeted her?

Logically, she felt certain the shooting was related to Emily's kidnapping. But what bothered her about both shooting attempts was that she and Doug had been near her well-marked-for-everyone-to-see Sullivan K9 SUV. Granted, the first shooting was at Doug's hotel, and this was at Emily's home, but in both instances, her SUV had been sitting out in plain view.

Were they wrong about the shooter's motive? Doug seemed to believe one of the perps he'd put away was seeking revenge. But really, it could just as easily have been one of the bad guys she had put away who was responsible for doing the same thing.

She hadn't imagined the guy popping up behind her for the past two weeks. Not on the ranch, but she'd noticed him in town. Every time she'd turned intending to confront him, he'd slink away.

Initially, she'd wondered if her ex-husband, Blaine Walter, had moved to Cody from Cheyenne where they'd lived together, but a call to the manufacturing company confirmed Blaine was still working in the area. It was such a long drive from Cheyenne to Cody, she doubted he'd have gone back and forth.

If not Blaine, though, then maybe someone she'd arrested. It wouldn't be impossible for one of the criminals she'd put away to find her here. The crime rate in Cody was low, but Cheyenne as the largest city in the state, plus the state capital had more criminal activity. She and her former K9 partner Ranger had put away several bad actors who'd committed crimes up to and including murder.

That had been a solid five to ten years ago, but for some people, prison could make a perceived wound fester.

"Maya? Something wrong?" Doug asked. She belatedly realized he was staring at her intently, as if trying to read her thoughts.

Giving herself a mental shake, she forced a smile. "No. I'm fine. Are you ready to go?"

"Yes, although I changed my mind about going to Cheyenne. Emily was taken from Cody. I think it's better to send the evidence to Cheyenne." He eyed her thoughtfully. "You mentioned a plane. Can I hire one to deliver a package?"

She nodded. "Sure, if you're willing to pay."

"Great. Let's go that route, then."

"I know a guy who flies charter planes in Greybull," she said. It was not the same owner of the plane that had crashed with her parents on board, as he'd died in the crash too. "Should only take an hour to get there."

"That works for me." He moved toward the damaged front door. "I hope your SUV wasn't hit."

"It wasn't." She had checked that out after Zion had found the shell casings. That had sparked the question as to whether she was the real target. She opened the back hatch, and Zion nimbly jumped in. "Interesting that this time the shooter's aim was better. All six shots hit the front door."

"Yeah, I noticed." He scowled as he slid into the passenger seat. After she'd started the car, he added, "I can't figure out what their endgame is. If they want to kill me, then why kidnap Emily?"

She had to wait for the police cruisers to move before she could back out of the driveway. Only once they were on the road heading toward the highway that would take them east to Greybull did she glance at him. "You know, I was a cop, too, so it could be that these shooters are after me."

"You?" He looked puzzled. "I don't understand what brought you to that conclusion."

She suppressed a sigh. She hadn't mentioned the guy she'd caught lurking behind her to her brother Chase. Or any of her other siblings. "I've noticed someone following me over the past two weeks. He's never shown up on the ranch, but he often materializes when I'm in town. We tend to use Cody for groceries and such because it's bigger and slightly closer than Greybull."

"So you've only seen this guy in Cody? Nowhere else?" He seemed genuinely concerned. "Do you have a description of him? Does he look like the shooter?"

"He's not Hispanic," she admitted. "But everyone is bundled up in the winter, so it's not easy to see facial features and body structure. And we know there were two men in the Silverado, one driver and one passenger who fired the shots."

"We'll need to go through your old case files along with mine," he said. "I still think that the shooter is related to Emily's disappearance, but we'll need to find this stalker dude of yours too."

"I'm fine. The guy slinking around me has never done anything—well, until now. If the shooter is the same guy." The more she considered the possibility, the less she liked it. Why had she even brought it up? She waved a hand. "Never mind. I think we should focus on your drug dealers and cartel members."

"I have put several cartel members away," Doug said thoughtfully. "They weren't all Hispanic, but some were. Milwaukee isn't close to the border, but the Great Lakes has been used to move drugs from one city to the next, the major hub being Chicago."

"I had no idea. Although it makes sense." She glanced at the majestic mountains looming up ahead. "I can't imagine living in a city as large as Milwaukee. I don't miss Cheyenne at all. And that's small in comparison."

"It's very different than here, that's for sure," he said with a wry smile. "What made you leave your job as a cop to do search and rescue?"

"My parents died in a plane crash five years ago." She didn't really like talking about it, but considering the hour-long drive ahead of them, there was no way to avoid it. "I moved home first, and my brother Chase followed. Soon, the rest of the siblings returned too." She hesitated, then said, "Chase is a year younger than I am. Then there's my sister Jessica, my brother Shane, sister Alexis, the twins, Joel and Justin, Trevor, and then Kendra, the youngest. She was only seventeen when our parents died, and we wanted to support her."

"Wow. And does each of your siblings have a dog too?"

"Yep. Chase is partnered with Rocky, Jess has Teddy, Shane works with Bryce, Alexis has Denali, Joel has Royal, Justin has Stone, Trevor works with Archie, and Kendra is partnered with Smoky."

"I'm sensing a national park theme," he said with a smile. "Is Stone short for Yellowstone?"

"It is, yes. The park theme was my idea, and training our dogs gave us something to work on together as a family in the aftermath of losing our folks." Her smile faded. "It's been hard but rewarding work."

"Humbling to know your entire family has focused on search and rescue." He reached over to touch her sleeve. "You did great, Maya."

His kind words made tears prick at her eyes, although she quickly blinked them away. She wasn't a crier, unless it came to the dogs. Ridiculous to let Doug's admiration get to her.

He was very different from Blaine. Maybe it was partially because he worked in law enforcement too. Or maybe Blaine was just that much of a jerk. Looking back, she could see now that her ex-husband hadn't been very supportive even at the beginning of their marriage. Why he'd proposed was a mystery, but then again, she'd been stupid enough to believe he was committed to her. And to having a family.

Wrong on both counts.

Whatever. Blaine was old news, and she had bigger issues to deal with. First and foremost, finding Emily.

The sound of Doug's stomach growling made her smile. She arched a brow. "Hungry?"

"Starved," he admitted. "Lunch is on me, remember?"

"That's not necessary," she said, but he held up a hand to stop her.

"I insist." He gazed out at the frozen landscape. "You know this area better than I do. How long before we reach civilization where we can get a meal? I'm not too picky, even fast food will do."

"We'll reach the next town soon," she said, glancing at

the fuel gauge. "It's about the halfway point. I'll fill up with gas then too."

"I'll do that," Doug said. "It's my fault we're driving out here in the first place."

She suppressed a sigh. "Thanks, but I can handle it. I already told you; the fee is a bag of dog food. I failed to mention we prefer a high-end natural dog food, so it's rather pricey."

He shot her an exasperated look. "I could give you ten bags of the highest priced dog food on the planet, and it wouldn't be enough. You've been shot at twice. I don't like knowing you and Zion are in danger because of me."

"Ten bags are too many," she said, trying to change the subject. "I'll settle on nine. That's one bag for each of our dogs."

"Then I'll make it eighty-one bags," he shot back. "I'm being serious here. I feel like I'm keeping you from doing real work." He stared out the window for a moment. "I doubt we'll find Emily along the highway, although you did mention those remote cabins and places to hide out."

"It's possible she was taken to Greybull," she said. "We should keep an eye out for that black Silverado."

"I have been." His expression turned somber. "I wish you and Zion weren't in the line of fire, though."

"Doug, I'm a trained cop turned search and rescue responder," she said calmly. "If I didn't want to be here, I wouldn't have offered to drive you. The reason I use my vehicle is because we have specially built-in safety measures. The car will start automatically if the temperature gets too low or too high. I can release Zion from the back from a distance if needed. And there's a water reservoir in the back for long trips, not to mention other search and rescue gear stashed under the back crate area." She glanced at him. "My car, my dog, my responsibility."

He didn't look happy, but the information about her SUV seemed to intrigue him. "This vehicle can really do all of that?"

"Yes. And the other nine SUVs we have on the ranch are equipped the same way. We have four-wheelers and snow machines, too, but they don't have these amenities. Zion isn't a huge fan of the snow machines, but she'll ride in front of me if I ask her to."

"Now that's something I'd like to see," he teased. Then he frowned. "Nine specialty vehicles, nine dogs, a big ranch. Sounds like it takes a lot of financial capital to keep your operation going."

"We manage." She was not going to discuss the ranch's financials with him.

He looked as if he might pursue the subject, then abruptly straightened when he saw the road sign indicating they were five miles from the next town. "Is that where we're getting lunch?"

"Yes." She couldn't help but smile at his enthusiasm. "They have a restaurant/truck stop named the Rolling Stone. The name is in reference to rocks that fall down the mountain, not the music group."

He chuckled, and she was almost annoyed to note that Doug was even more handsome when he laughed. Why she was so aware of him, she had no clue. It wasn't like her to be distracted by a guy. "Of course, it's not related to the music group. Seems country western is the only type of music anyone listens to out here."

"You've got that right." She slowed the SUV to turn off the highway.

Five minutes later, she pulled up in front of the Rolling

Stone restaurant. There were three other vehicles parked in the lot; none were a black Silverado. She'd kept an eye on the rearview mirror after leaving Cody and was confident they weren't followed.

Out here in the middle of no man's land, it was generally easy to spot a tail.

She opened the back hatch. Having been asleep, Zion opened her blue eyes, then popped her head up to see where they were. Maybe it was Maya's imagination, but the K9 looked sad they weren't home on the ranch. Having nine dogs meant lots of playtime.

Sometimes too much playtime.

"Come, Zion," she said. The dog didn't hesitate to jump down and stretch.

"You're taking her inside with you?" Doug looked almost disappointed, and she realized he'd wanted to see the K9-equipped SUV in action.

"Yes. Trust me, the owners won't mind." She didn't know them personally, but her brother Joel had done some work for them about eighteen months ago, when a kid had gone missing. Small towns loved to talk, and she knew the Sullivan K9 Search and Rescue name was widely recognized in the entire state, even as far as Idaho and Montana.

Entering the restaurant, they were greeted by a woman with brassy blond hair. "Welcome. Have a seat, I'll be over in a few."

Zion sniffed the area with interest, her tail wagging. The few customers inside smiled and nodded. She pretended not to hear how some of them whispered her last name, likely because Zion's vest had Sullivan K9 embossed on the side.

They shrugged out of their winter coats, took off their hats and gloves, then settled in a booth with Zion stretched out on the floor at her feet. The husky promptly went back to sleep with an ease Maya sorely envied.

The brassy blonde's name was Joyce, and she quickly came to get their order. Doug barely glanced at the menu, and she suspected he may have made up his mind long before they got there. Ever the gentleman, he gestured for her to go first.

"I'll have the chicken sandwich," she said. "With fries."

"That sounds good, except I want a cheeseburger with my fries," he said with a smile. "And coffee, please."

"For me too," she agreed.

Joyce nodded. "I'll have those meals out soon," she promised.

They were silent while Joyce returned with their coffee. As the hour was now past noon, Maya figured she might need to call Anna, their housekeeper, to let her know it wasn't likely she would be home in time for dinner. By the time they got back to Cody, she'd need to figure out a place for Doug to stay.

Someplace that was not on the Sullivan K9 ranch.

When she picked up her coffee cup, Doug reached over to lightly grasp her hand. "Thank you, Maya," he said.

"Ah, you're welcome." She avoided his gaze, far too aware of the tingling awareness that shot through her at his touch.

Not good. The last thing she needed was to be attracted to a man who was going to leave the moment they found his sister.

Wrong place, wrong time, wrong man. And the sooner she could convince her brain to ignore her attraction to him, the better.

5
———

Unnerved by the sudden awareness sizzling between them, Doug released Maya's hand. What was that about? Doug had been married what seemed like eons ago, divorced for nearly ten years. His wife had claimed she didn't love him anymore after three years of being together. He hadn't fought her on the divorce because he'd been forced to admit his feelings for her had changed too.

At the time, he'd decided they'd been too young for a lifelong commitment. But maybe the truth was that they weren't right for each other. Either way, he hadn't met anyone who'd interested in him enough to try again.

Maya intrigued him. Yet the moment that thought flitted through his mind, he ruthlessly thrust it aside. Emily was missing. He had no business thinking about anything other than finding his sister.

He sipped his coffee, avoiding Maya's gaze. It was troubling that his only plan consisted of getting the evidence to the state crime lab. There had to be something more he could do. Another lead to follow up on.

But what? Staring out the window at the sparsely populated town didn't provide any answers.

Joyce strode toward them carrying a platter in each hand. He sat back, setting his coffee aside to make room on the table.

"Here you go," she said cheerfully. One trait that had struck him since coming to Wyoming was how happy people appeared to be. There was no hustle or bustle rush-hour traffic unless it was caused by moose or elk blocking the road. Just a relaxed appreciation for life. "Enjoy."

"Thank you." He flashed a smile, despite his despair over his inability to find Emily.

Maya clasped her hands in her lap and bowed her head. He'd been around the Finnegans and Callahans enough to know she was saying grace, so he stared down at his lap, waiting for her to finish. When she lifted her head, a flush crept across her cheeks when she realized he'd noticed.

He picked up a french fry, then glanced beneath the table. "I take it Zion doesn't get table scraps."

"No, she doesn't, so don't even try." A wry smile tugged at her mouth. "The food we're eating is hardly healthy for us, much less my dog. But this rule is more about training. I can't allow Zion to be distracted by food while working. She knows she gets fed twice a day, and I try to keep her on a set schedule."

"Training a K9 sounds complicated." He thought about Miles Callahan and his K9 partner, Duchess. The two worked together as one, but he hadn't appreciated how they'd gotten to that point. "I wouldn't have considered the possibility of a dog being distracted by food."

"Not so much complicated, but consistency is key." She took a bite of her chicken sandwich. "We've been blessed with an amazing cadre of dogs. Different breeds, but each phenomenal in their skill and ability."

It would be amazing to see them all in action, but he would settle for Zion finding Emily. If they had some clue as to where to look. His idea of searching hotels had worked, and he thought again about why the Hispanic man had taken the bedsheets. If the reason was to avoid anyone obtaining his DNA, then he was likely in the system.

Which reminded him of the need to call his boss.

As soon as they finished eating, he set cash on the table to cover their bill. "I need to make a quick call before we head out."

Maya shrugged. "I'll take Zion out back to get busy."

He pulled out his phone and walked to a corner of the restaurant. It didn't take long for Special Agent in Charge Donovan to answer. "Are you calling from the plane?"

"No, sir. I didn't make my flight. My sister, Emily, went missing early this morning."

"Missing?" He could hear the doubt in his boss's tone. "She's an adult, isn't she?"

Suppressing a sigh, he quickly filled Donovan in on the details of his investigation. Upon hearing about the gunfire incidents, Donovan whistled.

"Sounds like your sister was used to get to you," his boss said.

"That's what I'm thinking," he admitted. "I need to take more vacation time, and I'm hoping you won't mind if I use Ian for help in running evidence."

There was a brief hesitation. "Technically, you shouldn't be working the case," Donovan finally said. "You're too close to this, Bridges."

He'd been expecting that comment. "With all due respect, sir, there isn't a plethora of federal agents in

Wyoming. There are three satellite offices spread across the state, but that's about it. And as far as I can tell, there are only one or two agents to cover them. I need to do this. I'm confident I can find Emily with help from a K9 search and rescue team. All I need is tech support from Ian and a quick turnaround on processing evidence."

Another pause, then Donovan sighed. "Fine. You can take your vacation time and use whatever resources you need. But I expect you to keep me updated on your investigation. There may not be a lot of agents out there, but they know the area better than you do. You may want to bring them in on the search sooner than later."

"Thank you, sir." He personally thought Maya's knowledge of the area, combined with Zion's expert nose, was far more valuable than an agent or two. But this wasn't the time to argue. "I'll be in touch."

His next call was to Ian Dunlap, their tech guru. When Ian answered, Doug got straight to the point. "I need you to run a list of perps I put away that have recently gotten out of prison. My sister is missing, and one of the perps is Hispanic, which may indicate a connection to the Robles drug cartel." It had been eighteen months since Doug had assisted Quinn Finnegan and his wife, Sami, in taking down several players within the Robles Mexican cartel. He put a hand to the now-healed bullet wound in his shoulder, a stark reminder of how close he'd gotten to being killed.

"I'm sorry to hear about your sister," Ian said. He could imagine the tech specialist playing the keyboard—like some musicians strummed a guitar—while using all four of his computer monitors. "I'll get that list run ASAP."

"Great, send it via email once you've complied it." He didn't want to think about how long the list might be. "Time is of the essence, Ian. She's been gone almost six hours, and I'm out of leads."

"Thanks to computer technology, it won't take long," Ian said reassuringly. "You'll see."

"Thanks again." He ended the call, then turned to head outside.

To his surprise, Maya and Zion were playing in the parking lot. Maya tossed a ball high into the air, and Zion gracefully leaped up to capture it in her mouth. He was amazed at the husky's gracefulness and agility. "Playtime?" he asked.

"Zion is high energy," Maya said, her cheeks red from the cold wind. "Are you set?"

"Yes." He waited until she told Zion to get into the back hatch before sliding into the passenger seat. She filled up with gas, refusing to use his credit card. When he thought of her eight siblings and nine dogs, he couldn't imagine why she didn't charge more for her services.

Then again, maybe it was a Christian thing. He had learned more about faith and God from the Finnegans and Callahans than he ever had from visiting a church. Interesting that Maya had similar views.

Not for the first time, he wondered if he was missing something.

Moments later, they were back on the slick highway.

The wind was stronger along this stretch of the highway, maybe because they were between the mountains. Gusts of snow blew across the road, but not badly enough to obscure Maya's vision.

Still, the SUV bucked beneath her fingers.

"I can drive if you get tired," he offered.

"I'm fine." She glanced at him. "Don't take it personally, but my dog is my responsibility."

"Precious cargo," he agreed with a nod.

They fell into a long silence as her SUV ate up the miles. When his phone vibrated with an incoming email, he was grateful to see Ian's name as the sender. Sensing Maya's curious gaze, he tapped the screen, opened the attachment, and used his thumbs to enlarge the document so that he could read it.

The list was longer than he'd anticipated, which was a poor testament to the legal system. Most of the perps he put away should be doing life without the possibility of parole. In his opinion, anyone poisoning children with drugs deserved to rot behind bars.

Obviously, with the ten names on the list, that wasn't the case.

"I have the names here of ten perps I put away for drug crimes," he said, filling Maya in on her unanswered question. "These are the ones who've been released from prison over the past six months." He hated to imagine how many would be included if he'd asked Ian to go back even farther.

"That's a good place to start," she said. "How many of them are Hispanic?"

"Six of the ten. Although I'm not sure I should eliminate the other four based on race. For all I know, the shooter himself is white." He ran his eye down the names. Two stood out as the highest potential for wanting to seek revenge. "My top suspects at this point are Horacio Cortez and Christopher Nolan."

"Remind me to make a call to the Cheyenne police department to get a similar list," Maya said. "Just in case this is about me."

He hated thinking about some creep following her around town. "You really don't have any idea who may be nursing an obsession with you?"

"No." She shrugged. "It's been a long time since I've been a cop. Even if someone I put away is upset and focused on me, why risk coming after me after all this time?"

"Anger can be a powerful motivator. And emotions are rarely logical."

The corner of her mouth quirked up in a cute smile. "True."

He wanted to ask more about her career but reminded himself to stay focused on the task at hand. He'd use this time to dig into the names Ian had sent. Reaching into the back seat, he retrieved his laptop and used his phone as a hotspot to connect to the internet.

The work was painstaking and frustrating. He didn't possess Ian's technical expertise. He finally discovered the names of each Cortez's and Nolan's parole officers. He punched each number into his phone, then made the calls. Both went to voice mail.

He sighed. Pressing his palms against his eyes, he hoped he was doing the right thing by sending the evidence to Cheyenne via plane rather than taking it himself.

Yet he couldn't afford to leave Cody for that length of time. Emily had gone missing from Cody.

He desperately needed to believe they'd find her in that area. And soon. A glance at his watch made him wince.

She'd been gone six hours and twenty minutes.

∼

Maya made good time getting to Greybull. When she reached the city limits, she found the road that would take her to Logan Fletcher's house. Logan often loaned his plane for search and rescue missions, which she and her siblings appreciated.

They all knew Logan had a keen interest in Jessica.

The road was rough, and Zion bounced in the back cargo area. She had been sleeping, but now she looked out with interest.

"Is that the place?" Doug asked, gesturing to the dark cabin with a dark plume of smoke rising from the chimney.

"Yes. Logan's plane is in the hangar." She gestured to the outbuilding that was twice the size of the cabin.

"You sound close," Doug said, glancing at her. Was it her imagination, or was there a hint of disappointment in his gaze?

Not important, she reminded herself. "Logan has used his plane to help us in a few search and rescue missions," she said. "He's a nice guy."

Doug nodded and looked away.

As she brought the vehicle to a stop, the front door opened, and she saw Logan standing there. She lifted a hand and noticed a flash of disappointment in his gaze that she was the one who'd come rather than Jessica.

"Hey, Logan," she called as she slid out of the driver's seat. "We need a favor."

"Come in," he said, stepping back. "It's freezing out here."

She released Zion from the back so the dog could tag along. Doug took a minute to pull the large bag of evidence from the back seat before joining her in entering Logan's home.

"How's Jessica?" Logan asked as she shut the door behind them.

She smiled. "Doing well. You could ask her yourself, you know."

The tips of Logan's ears turned red. "Just curious. That last case we worked was a tough one."

"I know. But we found the hiker, which is what matters." She put a hand on Doug's arm. "Logan, this is DEA Agent Doug Bridges, and we need your help in getting this evidence to the Cheyenne state crime lab as soon as possible."

Logan's expression grew concerned. "Of course. What's going on?"

"My sister went missing early this morning, and we've been targeted by gunfire several times," Doug said. "I'm happy to pay your going rate if you can get this to Cheyenne before the crime lab closes for the day."

"Of course. Any idea where your sister is now?" Logan asked.

"No." Doug swallowed hard. "We have two suspects driving a black Silverado with mud covering the license plates. That's it. Well, other than these bullet fragments and shell casings that were found with Zion's help."

Logan nodded. "The Sullivan K9s are impressive." The pilot glanced toward her, then back to Doug. "Happy to help. It should only take about two hours to get there, so I should be able to make it in time. And I'll charge you the Sullivan rate."

Doug's jaw dropped. "Dog food?"

Logan laughed. "No, I'll charge you what I charge them, only the cost of my fuel."

Maya knew Logan was doing that in hopes the word of his cooperation would reach Jessica. Although why he didn't just ask her sister out was a mystery. It wasn't like Jess was seeing anyone these days.

Doug gratefully paid the fee, adding an extra hundred for the expedited service. Logan shrugged and took the cash.

"Do you have paper?" Doug asked. "I'd like to document

the fact that I'm transferring ownership of the evidence to you. And in return, you would sign it over to the state lab." He shrugged. "It's the best I can do as far as validating the chain of evidence."

Ten minutes later, Doug had drafted the document, which was then signed by him and Logan. Then they exchanged phone numbers so Logan could call and let him know when the evidence had been received by the lab.

"Thanks very much," Doug said, offering his hand to Logan. "I'm grateful for your help."

"Anytime." Logan turned back to her. "Let Jess know I said hi."

It wasn't easy not to roll her eyes. "Sure thing. Take care, Logan."

She and Doug left the cabin, the biting cold stealing their breath. After getting Zion into the back, she and Doug settled up front.

"I take it that guy has a thing for your sister?" Doug asked with an arched brow.

"Yep." There was no point in denying it. Doug was a federal agent trained in reading people. And Logan, bless his heart, wasn't difficult to read. "Not sure why he doesn't just fly to the ranch and ask her out."

"He's probably afraid of being rejected," Doug said with a grin. "Believe me, most men are."

"Then he doesn't deserve to have her," she shot back.

"Ouch," he said with a chuckle. "But you're right. He needs to man up and ask her out."

"Yeah, while leaving me out of it," she muttered.

"Thanks again for driving me here," Doug said. "I feel better knowing the evidence will get to the lab by the end of the day."

"I'm glad." She left the long driveway to make the drive

back to Cody. "I was thinking that the best way for you to get a hotel room is for me to pay for it. You can pay me back," she hastily added the minute he opened his mouth to object. "But that's a better option than staying at Emily's."

"I hadn't thought that far ahead," he confessed. "It's killing me that we don't have another lead to follow. Other than trying to find the Silverado."

"Yes, I know." She squashed the urge to invite Doug for dinner at the ranch. Not smart. "Maybe you'll get some answers from the parole officers."

"Maybe." He grimaced. "I'll take you up on that offer of obtaining a hotel room. I guess I'll drive around Cody myself to see if I can find the truck."

She frowned. "By yourself?"

"I can always call the Cody PD for backup if I spot it," he said with a shrug. "Better than sitting in the hotel room waiting for a phone call."

He had a point. She wasn't much for sitting around either. Not that she intended to ride along with him on his mission of finding the truck. She'd already gone well out of her way to help him.

Oh, who was she kidding? She may as well tag along at least for a few hours. If they did find the truck, Zion would be able to track Emily's scent.

Letting them know if Emily had been inside.

The drive back to Cody seemed to take much longer than an hour. Maybe because they were both lost in their thoughts. Overhead, dark clouds rolled in from the west bringing the threat of more snow.

When they reached Cody, she drove to the Elk Lodge, the nicest hotel in the city. "Wait here," she told Doug. "I'll get the room, then we'll head over to grab your car."

"Thanks." He pushed more cash into her hand. "I'll stop at an ATM to get more later."

The man was obsessed with paying his way, but she took the money and headed inside. The clerk didn't hesitate to give her a room; although, she required Maya to use a credit card.

She handed Doug the key when she returned to the SUV. "Where do you want to start searching for the Silverado?"

His green eyes reflected gratitude. "You know the city better than I do. If you wanted to hide someone, where would you go?"

It was a good question, and she took a moment to think about it. She hadn't patrolled the city the way she had as a cop in Cheyenne, but she knew the type of neighborhood he was referring to. Apparently, they were similar in nature across the country. "There are a few abandoned places outside the northeast side of town. I suggest we start there."

"Let's do it." He appeared relieved to have a plan.

She put the SUV in gear and turned to head back the way they'd come. When she reached the highway outside of town, she turned north.

They patrolled the area for twenty minutes. She was about to turn back since they were well outside the city limits when she spotted a pair of tire tracks veering off the highway and heading into a wooded area. The recent snowfall indicated they were recent.

"Maya, is there a road there?" Doug asked, having noticed them too.

She tried to think. "Maybe an old dirt road, but I've never taken it, so I can't say for sure."

His gaze sharpened. "It's not that deep, can we head down it? See if we find anything?"

With a nod, she stopped, backed up, and turned to follow the tracks. She put the SUV into four-wheel drive. The road, if that's what she was on, seemed to be in decent shape.

Fully expecting to come upon a house in the woods, she hit the brake when she saw a truck with frost covering its windows.

A black Silverado truck with an obliterated rear license plate.

6

They'd found the truck! Doug bailed from Maya's SUV before she even came to a complete stop. His heart thundered in his chest as he ran toward the truck, his booted feet slipping in the snow. It was clearly abandoned, but he needed to make sure they hadn't left Emily inside.

Don't be dead, he thought as he wrenched the passenger door open. *Please don't be dead!*

He blew out his breath, making a cloud of steam when he saw the interior of the vehicle was empty. He peered over into the back seat to make sure.

Then, still braced for the worst, he turned toward the truck bed. His stomach clenched with dread as he used a gloved hand to push back the sliding cover.

Empty.

His shoulders slumped with a mixture of dejection and relief. The only good news was that he hadn't found Emily's dead body.

But the abandoned truck also meant they had nothing to go on. No way of finding his sister or the gunmen. The perps had left the vehicle prior to the local police spotting it and pulling them over.

"Doug?" Maya's voice broke into his thoughts, reminding him that he had one avenue to pursue.

He turned to face her. "Will you ask Zion to search for Emily?"

"Of course," Maya said without hesitation. "But come inside the SUV for a moment. We can't just run off into the woods without a plan. It's cold, and I need to make sure Zion is protected."

"Okay." He tamped down his impatience as he hurried back to the SUV. His passenger door was still open, so he slid into the seat and closed it.

Maya joined him, shutting the door against the chilly wind. The engine was still running, and he was grateful for the heat blasting from the vents. As his face warmed, he realized what she meant. Searching the woods in freezing temperatures was far different from spending a few minutes outside the hospital or the handful of hotels. He was desperate to find Emily, but not at Maya's or Zion's expense.

"Do we need to head back to the ranch so you can get more supplies?" He turned in his seat to face her. "I'm clueless as to what sort of gear you need to perform an outside search in temperatures like this."

"I have what I need for a thirty-minute search," she said. "I have booties for Zion, not that she likes them, and a face mask for me. The downside is that I don't see a set of footprints leading away from the truck to the woods. It's windy, so some of the snow could have blown over to cover them, but I don't see any indentations."

He glanced out the windshield, angry with himself that he hadn't noticed that detail. "You're right. There aren't."

"I don't want you to get your hopes up," Maya said softly.

"But I believe one of the gunmen drove this truck into the woods, walked back toward the road to be picked up by his cohort in crime."

It was easy to imagine the scenario she described. "Yeah, and if that's the case, there's no reason for you to expose Zion to the cold. You stay here. I'll just take a look around." He moved to open his door, but she grasped his arm.

"Hold on. We need to know if Emily was in the truck at some point. Let me work with Zion first."

This was exactly what Donovan had been worried about. He wasn't thinking logically, the way he would on a normal case. He needed to control his emotions. With a nod, he managed a smile. "Thanks. That would be great."

She held his arm for a moment longer, then let go to shut down the engine. He waited until she pushed out of the car to do the same. When she opened the rear hatch, Maya said, "Stay."

Zion waited for Maya to hurry over. He watched with interest as she put the booties over each of Zion's paws. "Out," she said. The husky nimbly jumped into the snow. Maya then offered the dog some water. Zion only took two laps, her blue eyes intent on Maya's face.

Doug got the impression Zion was anxiously waiting to hear the search command.

"Emily," Maya said, offering the scent bag to her K9. "Are you ready? Let's search Emily."

Zion's tail wagged as if this was her favorite game in the world, and she lifted her snout to the air, sniffing intently. Maya brought up the hood of her winter coat and drew a face mask over her nose and mouth. Doug could relate, the wind seemed colder for some reason, and he could feel his cheeks reddening from the bite of the wind.

The K9 swept her nose over the ground but didn't alert.

She made a zigzag pattern, sniffing the area interest as she grew closer to the truck. After several long minutes, she stopped at the rear passenger door. Rather than sticking her nose into the snow, Zion lifted her head toward the door handle.

He wanted to run over and open the back door for the dog but waited for Maya. After a full minute, Zion sat in the snow, glancing over at Maya with her intense blue gaze.

"Good girl," Maya praised. But she didn't pull the bunny out just yet. "Heel."

The dog trotted to Maya's side.

"Stay." Crossing over to the truck, Maya opened the back passenger door, the front passenger door, then even went around to the other side to open the other two doors. Then she stood back and held her K9's gaze. "Search for Emily!"

Zion trotted forward, sniffing the same door she'd alerted at just minutes ago. She sniffed along the bottom, then pressed her nose into the foot well. Without hesitation, the dog leaped into the back seat, burying her nose against the cushions.

The K9 spent so much time in the back seat he wondered what had caught the dog's attention. Then Zion jumped out of the truck, sat as close to the door opening as possible, and stared up at Maya in an unmistakable alert.

"Good girl, Zion!" Maya pulled the bunny out and tossed it toward her dog. Zion launched herself up to grab the bunny, then ran playfully, shaking her head as if playing tug-of-war with an imaginary four-legged friend.

"We know Emily was in the rear seat of the truck," Maya said. "Zion completely ignored the two front seats; she was only interested in the back."

"I noticed." He crossed to the vehicle. Peering inside, he tried to imagine his sister being held back there. Maybe with her wrists bound. Or maybe not, if the perps had a gun. He didn't see any blood, which was a good sign.

There was a bit of a gap between the seats, though. Using his gloved hands, he pulled the stiff cushions apart to look more closely.

Something had been wedged into the crevice. With a frown, he removed his gloves and used his cold fingers to dig into the gap. Feeling something hard, he managed to grip it well enough to pull it free.

Emily's phone. He gaped in shock, recognizing the pale-pink case and the screen photo of the two of them taken in front of her Christmas tree.

He held it up for Maya to see. "Zion is amazing. She knew this was there and that the device belonged to Emily."

Maya didn't look entirely surprised. "Zion is incredible, I won't argue that. And I'm glad we have more proof that Emily was inside."

"Zion's nose is proof enough for me." Tucking Emily's phone into his pocket, he pulled his gloves back on and swept his gaze over the interior of truck. Was it worth checking for fingerprints?

Yes. He couldn't afford not to double-check. Some people don't wear gloves when driving, even in the winter. And he didn't know how long the gunmen had been using the vehicle.

He'd get the license plate and VIN number sent through the DMV database too. His earlier disappointment at finding the truck empty had vanished. There were still avenues to explore.

"We need to get the two crime scene techs out here," he said. "I want this vehicle tested for fingerprints and possible DNA. I don't see any blood or other bodily fluids, but I trust Bart and Cindy to look in obscure places."

"I'll call the Cody PD," Maya said. "They'll want to see this for themselves. And cancel the BOLO," she added.

That was the part that hurt the most. No BOLO meant no one was out there looking for his sister.

He turned and headed to the rear license plate. It wasn't easy to scrape away the frozen mud covering the numbers and letters. He pulled out his phone to take a picture, then hurried over to the front of the vehicle. He had to scrape the ice and frost away from the glass to see the VIN. Zooming in, he took a picture of that too. Then he quickly emailed both photos to Ian Dunlap, asking for the registration and ownership of the vehicle.

He stepped back, wishing there was more to go on. But as he scanned the area, he was forced to agree with Maya. There were plenty of animal tracks in the snow, but nothing that resembled the stride of a human.

Emily must have been taken to a specific location prior to the gunmen dumping the truck. Zion hadn't alerted on her scent anywhere but inside the truck.

He turned once more, sweeping his gaze over the scenic and oddly peaceful landscape. There was no sign of civilization. Just snow-covered trees with the majestic Bighorn Mountains standing tall in the distance.

Yet he couldn't shake the thought that maybe, just maybe, the place where they'd taken Emily was somewhere close by.

~

"Come, Zion." After making the call to the Cody police, Maya turned her attention to her partner. She waited for the husky to trot over, then she held out her hand. The dog regurgitated the bunny from her mouth with her tongue.

"Good girl." She was freezing, but Zion didn't seem bothered by the cold. At least, not yet.

When she saw Doug heading toward the trees, she frowned. "Hey." Her voice was muffled by the face covering, so she pulled it aside. "Doug! Where are you going?"

"Just checking," he shouted back.

Checking what? She tried to ignore the flash of irritation. He was holding up fairly well, despite the Silverado being a dead end. Since Zion seemed fine, she quickened her pace to catch up to him.

"Checking what?" She fell into step alongside him. Zion trotted along, sniffing everything with interest.

"Signs of smoke rising from a chimney," he said somewhat absently. "I guess I was hoping Emily was being held somewhere nearby."

"You can't cover the entire area on foot," she protested. "This isn't Wisconsin. There are acres and acres of open countryside out here."

"I know." He shot her a quick glance. "You should take Zion back to the SUV. We're waiting for the Cody police and the crime scene van to get here anyway. I won't be long."

She couldn't bring herself to leave him. Not just because he was a city dweller, but she understood his urgent need to find his sister. Keeping a close eye on Zion, she mentally gauged the time. They'd been outside for a solid fifteen minutes, and she didn't want to expose Zion for much beyond the thirty minutes she'd given him earlier.

Ten minutes, no more, she decided. Then she'd force him back to the SUV. Without a face covering, he had to be getting cold by now.

At the five-minute mark, he abruptly stopped and lifted his hand toward the east. "Is that smoke?"

She frowned and followed his gloved fingers. "Maybe.

But it's hard to tell how far away that residence is. Come on, we need to get back to the SUV. You don't want to get frostbite on your nose."

He covered his face with his gloved hand. "You're right, I don't. But after the cops get here, can we head east for a bit? See if we can figure out where the cabin is located?"

Suppressing a sigh, she nodded. "Fine. But not until we have a chance to warm up."

He stared off at the thin curl of smoke in the distance for a poignant moment, then reluctantly turned around. "Okay. You're right about the cold. I can hardly feel my fingers and toes."

She quickened her pace. "Come, Zion!" Her husky bounded toward them, her curled tail wagging playfully. While Zion didn't appear bothered by the snow and cold, she didn't want to wait until the dog lifted her paws in a way that indicated they hurt.

Using the key fob, she started the SUV so the interior would be warm by the time they were able to get inside.

It took another few minutes for her to remove Zion's booties and towel dry her K9's paws. When that task was finished, she stepped back, closed the hatch, and hurried to the driver's seat.

"Do you know the treatment for frostbite?" Doug asked, leaning forward and moving the vents so they blew directly into his face. "I'm kinda attached to my nose."

She couldn't help but chuckle. "I think you're fine, but you need a face mask. And not a hospital one, but a real covering made of thick wool. I probably have a spare buried in the compartment under Zion."

He nodded and proceeded to continue warming his face. "What's the temperature out there now?"

"A balmy eighteen degrees." She tapped the tiny reading

in the upper left-hand corner of the display. "But the wind chill is probably minus five."

"No wonder I'm cold," he muttered. Then he sighed heavily. "But I don't want to miss the opportunity to find Emily. Every hour that passes without us finding her..."

"I know." She was keenly aware of the statistics surrounding a missing persons case. "We can drive farther east once the officers arrive. What about Emily's phone? Do you think there's anything to find there?"

He leaned back into his seat. "I doubt it. I find it hard to believe Emily knew her kidnappers. I think it's more likely they pretended to need medical help, drawing her close, then grabbing her. The way she slid her phone deep into the crack between the seats was her way of letting me know she was there."

"You're probably right." The seat warmers were doing an admirable job of bringing her core temperature up. She stripped off her gloves and stuck her fingers under her thighs. "Is your tech buddy going to run the vehicle?"

"Yep." He stared out the windshield. "I never realized how difficult it would be to find Emily in this weather. As if fighting against the bad guys isn't hard enough."

"We'll find her," she said, hoping and praying it was true. "I'm surprised we found the truck. I feel like God is guiding us on the right path."

He turned as if to argue just as a Cody police cruiser pulled up behind her.

"Hold that thought," she said. Keeping the engine running, she drew her gloves back on, covered her face, and opened her door. "Thanks for coming."

Doug quickly joined them. He held up Emily's phone. "Zion found this between the seat cushions. We know Emily was inside, but the kidnappers obviously abandoned this truck for another ride."

"May I?" Officer Jones asked, taking the phone from Doug. He stared down at the photo of Doug and Emily posed together under the tree. "Who took the picture?" he asked, handing it back.

"We put the camera on a timer." Doug dropped the phone into his pocket. "I was hoping your crime scene techs would check for fingerprints and DNA."

"Yeah, sure," Jones agreed. "They finished at Wild Bill's an hour ago. They'll be here shortly."

"Thanks," Maya said. "We appreciate your efforts on this."

"We didn't find the truck, you did." Jones shrugged, then waved a hand. "This is technically outside our jurisdiction, but that's okay. We want to find Emily too. We've canceled the BOLO for the truck but have distributed her driver's license photo to all officers. We'll keep an eye out for her."

"Thanks." Maya knew the kidnappers wouldn't keep Emily in town where they may be spotted. Not if they'd gone to the trouble of wiping down the motel room, stealing bedsheets, and ditching the truck.

She hated to admit this was looking more and more like a professional job. Had members from the drug cartel really taken Emily to get revenge on Doug?

Or was there something more going on here?

Once Bart and Cindy arrived, she and Doug sought refuge inside the welcome warmth of her SUV. It suddenly occurred to her that Emily's phone being found inside the Silverado meant the shooters hadn't targeted her as she'd previously feared.

This was all about Emily. And Doug.

Her creepy guy was still out there, somewhere, but that

was a problem for another day. They needed to stay focused on Emily.

"How much gas do you have?" Doug asked, breaking the silence. "I insist on filling your tank at the next closest fuel station."

"I'm good for a while." She shifted the gearshift into reverse. "There are no gas stations out here, only in town. We'll drive east for a while before I take you back to the hotel."

He frowned but didn't argue. She understood his dilemma. Returning to the hotel was akin to giving up the search. She wanted to point out that the smoke in the distance probably belonged to a local resident but knew he wouldn't believe her until he was confronted with the truth.

She drove slowly along the winding narrow highway, searching for the origin of the smoke. Eyeing her fuel gauge, she decided to go fifteen miles before turning around to head back to Cody.

"It's killing me," Doug said softly. "Knowing she's out there somewhere, helpless and unable to escape is killing me."

"I know." She lightly touched his arm. "Try to keep your faith in God. He will get you through this."

His mouth tightened. "Easier said than done."

"Yes, just as it was for Jesus and his disciples," she agreed. "Jesus preached, performed miracles, and still there were many skeptics and doubts to His claim of being the Son of God. It was only after He was crucified and rose again that they believed."

He turned to look at her. "I never thought of it like that."

She tried to smile. "It's easy to get caught up in the moment, focusing on our specific needs rather than looking for strength from above."

He covered her hand with his. "Thanks. That helps a lot. I feel better. Although I won't be satisfied until I find her."

"Of course you won't." She was touched by his humble faith. "I won't either. But we can't drive around forever."

He grimaced and nodded. "I know this is probably a wild-goose chase. Just give me a few more minutes." He dropped his head and turned to stare back out the windshield. "I just want to follow up on that plume of smoke."

She couldn't blame him for hanging onto the thread of hope. If one of her siblings was missing, she would scour the entire state to find them.

Driving slowly, she tried to remember if she met anyone living in the area. Hadn't she and Zion been out here roughly two years ago? It had been early fall, and the current layer of snow made it harder to identify specific landmarks.

In truth, she'd been in so many different wooded areas it wasn't always easy to keep track. Even when using the individual mountain peaks as a focal point.

Doug's phone rang, startling them both. Zion opened one eye, then closed it again.

"Hey, Ian, what do you have?" Doug asked. His hopeful gaze turned grim as he listened. "I was afraid of that. I'm sure that's why they covered the license plate with mud. Thanks for trying. I'll call if I can come up with anything new."

"The truck was stolen?" she guessed.

"Yeah, here in Cody. Seems as if it was reported stolen late last night." He sighed and scrubbed his hands over his face in a defeated gesture. "I'm fine with heading back to the hotel. I'll work on pulling property information for land between Cody and Greybull. Maybe I can narrow down a few viable search areas. We should also consider looking at rental properties. Not that the bad guys would go through normal channels to obtain the space, but more likely they'd break in knowing no one was home. Those companies try to keep addresses secret, but there are ways around that."

"Good idea." She glanced at him. "I can help by identifying long-term residents. Not that I know them all, mind you, but ruling out a few of the properties will help narrow the list."

"Thank you." His smile was weary. "I honestly don't know what I'd do without you."

His comment shouldn't have made her blush. She kept her gaze focused on the road, hoping he wouldn't notice. "It's nothing, just our warm western hospitality."

"I'm serious, Maya." The force of his stare made her glance over at him. "You and Zion have been invaluable. I wouldn't have found the evidence of Emily being at the Wild Bill Motel or here in the truck without you."

"Zion is the star of the show," she said, trying to lighten the mood. When Doug frowned, she added, "You're welcome. But remember, search and rescue is what we do. I could never walk away from a missing woman." She hesitated, then said, "I'd ask my siblings for help, but at this point, there's nothing to go on. But if we can pinpoint a location, I'll bring them in to assist."

"Thanks, and I'll gladly take you up on that." He glanced out at the landscape. "I'm not sure why, but I get the sense she's close. Maybe not near the abandoned truck, but I don't think they've taken her far. If the goal is to entice me to come after them, or to give myself up in exchange for her release, then I wish they'd hurry up and contact me."

Her stomach clenched. "You can't offer yourself up in exchange for Emily."

"Oh yeah I can," he said without hesitation.

"Doug, they'll likely kill you both." She tried to hide the flash of panic. "Don't overreact. I'm sure we'll find a way to rescue Emily."

There was a moment of silence before he responded. "I'm not overreacting. And I don't have a death wish. However, if I get a ransom demand of some sort, all bets are off. I'll gladly exchange my life to save hers." He grimaced, then added, "But since I haven't heard from these guys, I'll keep searching for possible locations."

She nodded and pressed her foot down on the accelerator to increase her speed. His comment about sacrificing himself bothered her, more than it should have. She barely knew the guy, but the thought of him giving up his life was unacceptable.

The sooner they could narrow down a search field, the better. She had faith in God and in Zion's nose. They would find Emily.

She couldn't bear to consider the consequences if they didn't.

7

As Maya pulled into the parking lot of the Elk Lodge, Doug tried not to feel like a failure. He was a federal agent who couldn't find his own half sister. The cold and wintery conditions were only part of the problem. He needed to get his emotions in check long enough to take methodical investigative actions.

His attempt to locate a mystery plume of smoke from a car had been emotional and irrational. Time to focus on facts and data. In the past, he and Ian had successfully found bad guys by searching property records. He'd get Maya's assistance on that, and hopefully, he could ask Ian to dig into the list of ten names.

Maybe one of them had a sister, girlfriend, or wife that had suffered after being arrested. This could be some sort of warped eye-for-an-eye retaliatory response.

He turned to Maya as she killed the engine. "You don't have to stay if you have things to do. I can work out some possibilities and let you know what I find."

"I said I'd help." She shot him an exasperated look. "Let's go."

He was grateful for her stabilizing presence. Maybe it was just the fact that he didn't live in Wyoming and had no knowledge of the area other than what he'd gleaned over the past ten days of visiting with Emily, but he was acutely aware of how much he needed her.

Far more than he'd initially realized.

"Thank you." He pushed out of the car and grabbed his suitcase and laptop bag. Maya freed Zion from the back hatch, and together they headed for the door.

Inside, the lobby fire greeted them warmly. He took off his gloves, even though his fingers were still rather numb. Maya did the same, then pulled out the room key she'd obtained upon securing the room and handed it to him. He was a little surprised no one complained when they headed down the hallway to the room with Zion between them. He quickly unlocked the door and headed inside.

The room was decorated in a traditional western motif—pictures of wild animals on the walls, headboards made from logs. It was nicer than the Lumberjack Inn, not that he cared. He dropped the suitcase next to one of the double beds, then set the computer case on the desk. "Give me a minute to power this up," he said.

"Take your time." Maya was watching as Zion sniffed the room with interest. "I'll head out to grab Zion's food soon."

He nodded absently, plugging the laptop in to power it up. Then he reached for his phone to call Ian.

"Did you find her?" Ian asked.

"No." His chest squeezed painfully. "I need some help before you head home." He was aware of the time difference. "I need a list of property owners for Cody and Greybull, Montana. I may have to extend that at some point, but we'll start there. I also need help with digging into these ten perps who have recently been released from jail." He had to think back for a moment. "I left voice mails for the parole officers of my two top suspects, Horacio Cortez and Christopher Nolan, but haven't heard back." With all the excitement of finding the Silverado and Emily's phone, he hadn't noticed until now. "I'll call again, but it occurred to me that whoever took Emily may have a sister, wife, or girlfriend who suffered because of his arrest."

"That's a definite possibility," Ian agreed. "I'll send you the property list first, then dig into those ten names to look for any underlying motives that may be at play."

"Thanks so much," Doug said. "I can pay you overtime if needed."

"Don't be ridiculous," Ian said without heat. "I'm here for you."

His throat swelled with emotion. "Thanks again." He ended the call, feeling blessed at knowing he had great people to support him.

"Doug? Are you okay?" Maya crossed over to rest her hand on his shoulder.

The urge to stand, sweep her into his arms, and kiss her was strong. But he managed to refrain from making a fool of himself.

"Yes. Fine." He covered her hand with his. The skin-to-skin contact made his nerve endings tingle. But he told himself that was just his fingers starting to thaw. He let her go and shrugged out of his coat. "I think I mentioned our tech expert, Ian Dunlap. He's sending me that list of property owners. We'll start there."

"Sounds good. I need to grab some supplies for Zion from the back of the SUV," she said. "I won't be long."

He was about to turn back to his computer but hesitated. Hadn't she mentioned something about some guy stalking her? He rose. "I'll go with you."

"No need. I'd rather you stay here with Zion." She waved a dismissive hand. "This will only take a few minutes."

He frowned, but his phone buzzed with an incoming call from a 414 area code, which meant it was probably one of the parole offices calling him back. "Okay." He lifted the phone to his ear. "This is Agent Bridges."

"Officer Cotter, you called to ask about Chris Nolan?"

"I did, thanks for calling me back. My half sister has been kidnapped, and I'm trying to narrow the suspect field. I put Nolan away three years ago, but I've heard he is out on parole. Have you seen him lately?"

"Nolan, Nolan," Cotter muttered. Doug heard the clatter of fingers on a keyboard. "Oh yeah, here he is. Chris Nolan is one of my parolees, but it looks as if I haven't seen him in over a week."

A flash of excitement hit hard. "He's supposed to be seen weekly?"

"Yeah, for a pep talk and pee drug test," Cotter said. "I hadn't gotten around to tracking the paroles who are AWOL. I'll make a few calls, see if I can track him down. I'll also issue a warrant for his arrest."

"Thank you. Will you call me back if you find him?" Doug wasn't sure if the guy was strung out on drugs or if he had traveled halfway across the country to Cody, Wyoming. "My sister was taken from the hospital where she works in Cody, Wyoming, so I'm not there to help track him down."

"Wyoming?" Cotter sounded as shocked as if he'd said Mars. "Why in the world would Nolan head way out there?"

"To seek revenge." It sounded weak, but he didn't have anything else to go on. "Please keep me updated. Thanks." He quickly ended the call, then contacted the other parole office too. Still no answer, so he left another message, this one more urgent.

He stared at his computer screen, wondering how long it would take for Ian to send the list of property owners. Zion made a whining sound in her throat, causing him to glance over at her. The K9 sat by the door, staring at him.

"She'll be back soon," he said. Zion didn't even blink. When he turned to face the screen, she whined again.

He rose and walked toward her. "What is it?"

Her blue gaze held his, as if she were trying to tell him something but obviously couldn't say the words.

He glanced at his watch. Maya hadn't been gone that long. When Zion whined for a third time, he gave in and reached for his coat. "Okay, I hear you." Easier to meet Maya halfway than to ignore the K9's eerily intense stare and high-pitched whine.

"Let's go." He reached over the dog's head to open the door. Zion bolted from the room like a rocket without looking back. Alarmed, he quickly ran to catch up to the dog.

The husky stood at the front door of the lobby, her nose pressed against the glass. She let out a sharp bark, startling him. Zion rarely barked.

"What's wrong?" He pushed the door open, the blast of cold air stealing his breath. Zion snuck past him and took off.

Once again he ran after the dog, alarmed by the K9's actions. When he saw Maya's SUV in the parking lot with the back hatch lifted, his heart squeezed painfully when he realized she wasn't standing behind it.

"Maya!" he cried as Zion disappeared around the far side of the car. He quickly caught up, horrified to find Maya lying on the ground. "Maya! Can you hear me?"

Zion licked Maya's face, causing her to stir. She looked up at him in confusion, then gingerly pushed herself into a sitting position. He placed his arm around her back for additional support.

"Someone hit me," she said.

Doug silently thanked God for Zion's sense of danger. "Let's get you inside."

She didn't put up a fight as he put both of his hands beneath her arms and lifted her upright. She slumped against the SUV for a moment, before managing to stand on her own. "I'm fine."

She wasn't, but he saw what looked like a doggy backpack with the words Sullivan K9 Search and Rescue embroidered on the side, sitting just inside the open crate area. He slung the strap over his shoulder, slammed the hatch, then slipped his arms around her waist. "Lean on me. We need to get you inside."

This time she didn't argue. Zion stayed glued to Maya's side as they made their way back into the warm lobby. She did lean on him, but he noticed the fingers of her left hand rested lightly on Zion's fur too.

The room door hadn't completely closed behind him. He performed a quick search to make sure the room was empty. He gently nudged her down onto the bed, then set the doggy backpack on the floor.

"Where do you hurt?" He knelt beside her, unzipping her bulky parka and pushing it off. Then he pulled her knit cap off as well. There were no obvious signs of injury, but she was covered from head to toe.

"My head." She lifted a hand to gingerly palpate the back of her scalp. "He came up behind me. I sensed his movement and tried to get away, but too late. He hit me, and I stumbled forward." Her dark eyes clung to his. "I don't remember anything until you and Zion arrived. I guess I blacked out for a minute."

He kicked himself for letting her head out alone. "May I?" He rose to his feet and pushed her hand away to examine her head. Her brunette wavy hair was thick and soft. Then he felt the swelling toward the top of her head. "The skin isn't broken, but I'm sure it's painful."

"It is, but I'll survive." She grimaced. "I can't believe I let that guy get the drop on me."

"You didn't see his face?"

"Not really. A quick glimpse of dark eyes above his face mask." She thought for a moment, then added, "I'm positive he's a white guy, though. Not Hispanic."

"Could it be the same guy you've sensed following you before?" He pressed. "Same height and build?"

"Maybe." She sighed, lifted a shoulder, and said, "I never expected the man I've noticed slinking around to physically assault me. Granted, I usually have Zion with me, so maybe he caught a glimpse of me being alone and took the chance to take me out." She looked up at him. "I wouldn't have lasted too long in the cold. Thanks for coming out to find me."

"Zion forced the issue." He glanced at the husky stretched out on the floor beside the bed with admiration. "I'm not sure how she knew you were in danger, but she was extremely persistent."

"Good girl," Maya said, leaning over to stroke the dog's fur. Zion wagged her tail, glancing at him as if to say *I told you so*.

His phone buzzed with an incoming message. A quick glance confirmed Ian had sent the list of property owners. While thrilled to have a place to start, he couldn't help but wonder if this attack on Maya was an isolated event.

Or somehow connected to Emily's disappearance.

THE INCIDENT outside her SUV replayed in her mind as she pressed the ice pack Doug had insisted on making against her sore head. Was it the same guy she'd seen over the past two weeks?

She couldn't say for sure. Until now, he'd kept his distance. In fact, he'd always left her alone once she'd noticed and turned to look at him.

This assault—she winced. She had not anticipated it. And why had the guy turned violent after all this time?

It didn't make any sense. She couldn't imagine whom she could have angered enough to do something like this. Other than her ex-husband, who had gotten angry when he'd learned he could not cash in on her inheritance. Or any other financial support, considering he'd cheated on her and their marriage had barely lasted four years. The judge had outwardly viewed Blaine with disdain. She'd realized part of the judge's annoyance was because he knew full well they didn't take any cash payments for their search and rescue operations.

Could Blaine be involved? Maybe she had underestimated his level of anger and frustration. His anger could have festered over the years, especially since their search and rescue business had gotten so much great press.

She made a mental note to double-check her ex-husband's whereabouts in the morning.

"Are you sure you don't want to be seen at the hospital?" Doug scowled as he stood beside her, making her crane her neck to look up at him. "It's not smart to mess around with head injuries."

"I'm fine." Her head hurt, but it wasn't terribly bad. She didn't want to admit that part of her reaction to falling unconscious was probably sheer surprise at being struck in the first place. Obviously, some of her cop reflexes had gone slack. She'd believed that staying in shape by exercising the dogs and doing search and rescue would keep her sharp.

Until some lowlife jerk had cowardly hit her from behind.

She was irritated by her lapse in being aware of her surroundings, but all she could do was move forward from here. If Zion had been there, her K9 would have alerted her to the guy's presence.

And if she caught a glimpse of him again, she would send Zion after him. Her K9 specialized in tracking, but Zion was protective enough that if she gave the command to *Get him*, the dog would chase a perp down without hesitation. Zion's bark was worse than her bite, but he wouldn't know that.

Times like this, she missed her K9 Ranger. He was an extremely intimidating German shepherd who had been trained in suspect takedowns. Very similar to Shane's dog Bryce.

"I'd like you to stretch out and relax." Doug's voice interrupted her thoughts. He pulled back the covers on the bed. "I'm not a nurse like Emily, but I know the best treatment for a head injury is rest."

She swallowed a flash of impatience. As the oldest sibling, she was used to being in charge. She didn't appreciate being treated like a child. "You need to trust my judgment. I have had plenty of first aid training working search and rescue missions. I promise I'm not badly hurt. If my symptoms change for the worse, I'll let you know and go to the hospital."

He didn't look convinced, and the last thing she wanted was to be seen. People talked, and the news would spread to

Chase or her other siblings like lightning. Her family would make a big deal out of a little bump, and she wasn't in the mood to keep arguing.

"Do you want my help?" She tried not to sound as crabby as she felt. "Let's dig into that list of properties. Hopefully, we can narrow them to a few possible locations where these guys might be holding Emily."

He hesitated, clearly torn between accepting her help and insisting she climb into bed. "Only if you tell me if your vision gets blurry or you feel sick to your stomach."

"I promise. Let's work for an hour. I'll need to feed Zion about then, and we may want to order room service as well."

"Okay." He gestured to the single chair. "Have a seat."

"Pull the desk over so you can use the corner of the bed," she suggested. Having Doug leaning over her shoulder would be nerve-racking. "That way we can both see the screen."

With a nod, he set about rearranging the furniture. When he was finished, she took the chair as he perched on the end of the bed. He was still too close for her peace of mind, but she told herself to focus on the list of names on the screen.

It was longer than she'd anticipated, but that was partially because the addresses included all of Cody and Greybull, not to mention the outlying regions. A sense of despair hit hard. This felt like looking for gold in a defunct mine.

"What do you think of starting with those addresses that are not within the city central," Doug asked. "I'm not sure how to sort through them, though."

"Try sorting them by house number," she suggested. "That will help." She caught a glimpse of the last name of Pickard. "Maybe sort them in two ways, by last name and street number. I know a guy by the name of John Pickard owns several properties, many of them are rentals."

She closed her eyes for a moment as Doug manipulated the data. Her vision wasn't blurry, but concentrating on the names and numbers was making her head hurt. Not that she intended to mention that fact to Doug.

"Do you know this Pickard guy?" Doug asked. "Would he rent to criminals?"

"Not on purpose, but I don't think he'd ask too many questions either. If someone wanted to rent a house that was empty for a few days for cash, he'd take the money." She shrugged. "Most folks out here would. You have to remember that this is not a high crime area. Not like the big city."

"Yet Emily was kidnapped, and you were assaulted," he pointed out wryly.

"True." Hard to argue that one.

"Do the police know about your stalker?" he asked.

"No." She sighed as he stared at her. "I was a cop. There's nothing the Cody police could have done without a specific description to go on."

"They could have checked camera video." He arched a brow. "Are there any security cameras in town?"

"A few on the main traffic lights, but most businesses don't bother." She shrugged. "It's an unnecessary added expense when crime isn't a top concern."

"You're telling me you never run into criminal activity while doing your job?" His tone was skeptical.

She lowered the ice pack because her arm was growing tired of holding it. She glanced at Zion who was sleeping at her feet. "I can't say never, but it's rare. Most of our cases involve lost tourists who underestimate the wilderness or the weather or locals getting hurt while hunting or fishing."

"Okay, okay." He held up his hands. "I guess my installing a camera doorbell at Emily's was overkill."

She understood he'd gotten the camera out of concern for his sister's safety. A fear that proved to be well founded, considering her disappearance.

He held her gaze for a long moment, then turned back to the computer screen. "We have eight names of residents owning multiple properties," Doug said, picking up the thread of the investigation. "This Pickard guy owns the most. Then we have a man by the name of Timothy Worth who owns three places. The rest seem to own two properties. I assume one is a full-time residence; the other is more of a vacation property."

"Hunting land with a cabin most likely, although most people I know hunt public land as there's so much of it available." She leaned forward. "Hmm. I don't know Tim Worth. Our paths have never crossed, or he might be new to the area. The other names are familiar, and they're all men, which gives credence to the hunting cabin theory. In my experience, men with hunting and fishing land don't rent to strangers."

"Okay, lets focus on Pickard and Worth." Doug pulled up a map of the two cities up on the screen. "Can you help me pinpoint where their properties are on this map?"

She nodded and took a few minutes to find each of the address locations. "Every single one of Pickard's properties are in town, although it's interesting he has homes in both Cody and Greybull." She turned to look at him. "Since we found Emily's scent in the Wild Bill Motel, I don't know that we should bother checking them out."

He hesitated for a moment, then nodded. "Makes sense. If they had rented a house in town, there would be no reason to use the motel."

"They could have, but they may attract attention in town too. Let's see what Tim Worth has on file." She checked the first address and the second. Both were in Greybull. The third was a cabin outside of Cody. Interestingly, it wasn't that far from the location where they found the Silverado truck.

"Is that where I think it is?" Doug asked. "Near the abandoned truck?"

"Yes. It looks like there's a driveway from this other road, here." She tapped the screen, then glanced at him. "But you know this could just be a hunting cabin too. Just because I'm not familiar with Tim Worth doesn't mean he's connected to bad guys."

"I know, but maybe our bad guys stumbled across the place. They realized it was empty and decided to use it as a hideout."

"That possibility could apply to any of these properties," she felt compelled to point out. "Worth could be living in this house and renting the places in town."

His shoulders slumped. "You're right. I need to think this through." He looked so discouraged her heart ached for him. After a moment, he looked at her. "I'm not sure where to go from here. What do you think? Do I keep searching those properties around the abandoned truck? Or focus on rentals? It'll be dark soon."

She glanced out the window, somewhat surprised to realize he was right about the daylight. The hour was going on four thirty in the afternoon, and dusk was falling. She turned back to face him. "Let's look at the properties around the abandoned truck. We can head out to search them first thing in the morning."

He frowned and opened his mouth to say something, then caught himself. "Okay."

She quickly identified the two property owners within a

fifteen-mile radius of the abandoned truck. "Only two that I can see. Another four if we go out even farther," she said, sitting back in her chair. Her head was throbbing again, likely from her work on the computer screen.

They had six places total to check out come morning.

"That helps." Doug took over the keyboard to send the map she'd highlighted to his email. Then he rose to his feet. "I'll be back soon."

"No, wait." She quickly grabbed his hand to prevent him from going. "You can't go alone. If you get lost, you'll freeze to death."

His expression turned stubborn. "I'll use the compass on my phone. I can also call if I get lost or if something happens."

She narrowed her gaze, feeling just as stubborn. "Phones don't always work way out here; there are areas where cell tower signals don't reach."

"I'll take the risk." He spoke in such an offhand way she grew angry.

"That's a stupid risk." She jumped to her feet, startling Zion. Her K9 looked up at her, likely wondering if it was dinnertime. "And one that isn't going to help Emily if she is nearby, but you end up breaking your fool neck before finding her."

They stared at each other for a long, tense moment. Then without warning, he pulled her into his arms and kissed her.

8

Wow. He should not have kissed Maya. The rational thought that had flashed in his brain was quickly overpowered by sheer emotion. She was sweet and melted into his arms, kissing him back with an enthusiasm that made his heart race.

Then she abruptly pulled out of his arms. The grim expression on her face was like a kick in the teeth.

He regretted taking advantage of the situation. "I'm sorry, that was inappropriate. I shouldn't have crossed the line." He cleared his throat, willing his heart to settle down in his chest. "It won't happen again."

She drew in a breath and met his gaze. "No need to apologize. It was just a kiss. No biggie."

Ouch, he thought with a wince. He forced himself to take a step back, belatedly realizing Zion was standing near Maya's side as if ready to pounce on him if he made a wrong move. Swallowing hard, he quickly shoved his laptop into the carrying case and reached for his coat. "I'll be back soon."

"Wait." She grabbed his arm. "If you insist on going, I'll

come with you and bring Zion. But we will only work outside for twenty minutes. No longer."

He glanced at the looming dusk outside. "Twenty minutes," he agreed. "I don't want to place you or Zion in danger."

Releasing his arm, she turned toward Zion. She ran her fingers through the dog's thick coat. "We'll eat when we get back, okay?"

The husky wagged her tail as if understanding every word. At this point, the connection between Zion and Maya was so strong he didn't doubt their ability to communicate on a different level than most.

Maya drew on her coat and hat. Then she grabbed Zion's duffel.

"Do you need this?" He took the bag from her fingers. He'd snagged his laptop so he'd have the map, but he was surprised she was taking Zion's bag.

"Better to be prepared for anything." She shrugged and followed him toward the door. "We need to hurry. The light won't last long."

He nodded and held the door for her. They headed down the hall, through the lobby, and out into the frigid temps. It didn't take long for them to head back out on the highway toward the area where he'd seen the earlier plume of smoke.

The laptop was open, and he had the map of the area up on the screen. As he searched the side of the road for the location of the abandoned Silverado, he prayed he wasn't making another mistake. Darkness fell quickly out here, and he didn't want to risk anything happening to Maya or Zion. Yet the ticking clock in his head wouldn't let him rest. If they didn't find anything within the twenty-minute time frame, they'd have to wait until morning.

And Emily will have been missing twenty-four hours by then.

"There's where the Silverado was left behind," he said. The snow was matted down, and there were additional tire tracks that had been left by the police cruisers. Glancing down at the map, he could see the cabin was only a few miles from here.

"I see it." Maya kept going. "Tim Worth's cabin is north and east from this location. We need to get to the next intersection and take that road to search for a driveway."

He nodded, impressed with her knowledge of the area. "Sounds good."

When they reached the intersection, she slowed her speed to turn left. "Okay, keep your eyes out for any hint of a driveway."

The light was fading fast, but the snow helped provide some ambient light.

"There's no sign of a road or a driveway." Now that they were in the general location of where this cabin was supposed to be according to the map on his screen, he was assailed by doubts. "How would the kidnappers have gotten Emily to the cabin?"

"Lots of people use snow machines out here, but we'd see tracks." She frowned and pulled over to the side of the road. "Tim's place should be somewhere out there. We'll head out for a quarter mile or so. Unfortunately, I don't have any snowshoes with me."

He gazed at the blanketed landscape. He'd seen snowshoes in stores but had never used them. "All we can do is try."

"If the going gets too rough, we'll have to turn back." She held his gaze. "I mean it, Doug. It's too cold to mess around."

"I know. I'll follow your lead on this." He closed the

laptop and tucked it beneath the seat, silently admitting she was the expert when it came to the region.

"Give me a few minutes to get Zion set." She pushed out of the SUV, hit the button to raise the back hatch, then headed out into the cold wind. Since sitting there in the warmth seemed wrong, he quickly joined her.

"Are you ready to work, girl? Are you?" He noticed Maya put a note of excitement in her tone. The dog's blue gaze was locked on her face as she placed the snow booties over Zion's paws. Then she offered Zion a bit of water. After the dog took a lap or two, she offered the bag of Emily's clothing. "Emily. Search! Search for Emily."

Zion nimbly turned and lifted her nose to the wind. Maya closed the SUV, waiting for Zion to make a move. He found himself holding his breath as the K9 stood for a moment, then headed toward the woods.

Maya glanced at him as they hurried after the dog. He couldn't tell if Zion had found Emily's scent or not. The K9 didn't alert, so he assumed she was still searching for his sister's scent.

The last remnants of light disappeared less than five minutes into their walk. If not for the reflection of the moon and the stars off the snow, they'd be forced to turn back.

To his relief, Maya pushed on. Her twenty-minute deadline loomed before them, and he lifted his gaze to the sky.

Please, Lord Jesus, guide us to Emily!

The prayer didn't ease the tension as much as he'd hoped. He couldn't allow himself to think about what Emily might be suffering at the hands of the men who took her. He watched Zion as she darted between the trees.

They were almost at the ten-minute mark when he caught a glimpse of a cabin. "Maya?" He caught her hand, keeping his voice low. "Is that Tim Worth's cabin?"

"Looks like it," she whispered back. They paused near the trees as Zion moved closer. "I don't see any smoke coming from the chimney, though."

He didn't either. In fact, from what he could tell, the place hadn't been used recently. There were no footprints in the snow, no tire tracks.

Nothing.

And most importantly of all, Zion didn't alert on Emily's scent. After trotting around a bit, she returned to Maya's side and looked up at her as if asking for another command. The K9 clearly wanted to find Emily too.

He battled a wave of despair.

"We need to head back to the car," Maya said. "There's no point in getting any closer. Zion would have told us if Emily had been here."

He nodded and forced himself to turn away from the silent and still cabin. He should have known better than to believe Emily had been taken to a place that was so close to where the abandoned vehicle was found. She'd been taken from the Silverado and placed in another car.

And if the kidnappers were smart, they'd have driven far away from the dump spot.

Maybe even halfway across the state.

But why? That was the part of this that didn't make any sense. Why had some drug dealer he'd put in jail have taken Emily in the first place?

He was so lost in his thoughts that the tip of his boot caught a rock and sent him sprawling face first into the snow. Feeling like a fool, he quickly pushed himself upright, trying to brush the snow from his clothes.

"Are you hurt?" Maya asked.

"No." But the fact that he hadn't seen the rock reinforced why searching at night wasn't smart. "I'm fine."

As soon as the K9 SUV came into view, Maya used the key fob to start the engine and to open the rear hatch. As usual, she focused on taking care of her dog first. Reassuring Zion that she'd been a good girl and that it would be time for dinner soon.

"I'm sorry," he said, once they were settled in the SUV and heading back to Cody. "I shouldn't have insisted on coming out tonight."

She arched a brow. "Searching at night can be dangerous. But I'm glad we went. We found the cabin without difficulty and know now that Emily has never been there. We can cross that one off our list."

"Yeah." He couldn't seem to find satisfaction in that. He pulled the laptop from beneath the seat. "One down and hundreds of possibilities to go."

Maya didn't say anything for a long moment. "It's hard to know if tracking down rental properties is the right answer. These guys could be local. Or have ties to a local resident." She glanced at him. "Maybe you need to focus on those parolees. Is there a way to see if they've rented properties here? Can you get a search warrant for that?"

"Chris Nolan hasn't checked in, so yeah, I can probably get one for him." His heart lightened at the possibility.

He needed to be more methodical in his investigation. The clock was ticking, and every minute that Emily was gone, his chances of finding her lessened. But he needed to stay positive.

With Maya and Zion being there, he had an edge. One that he intended to use to his advantage.

If Nolan was their perp, he'd taken Emily for a reason. The same applied to Cortez.

He stared at the lights of the small city of Cody

spreading before them. Was she closer than he realized? Maybe.

He silently vowed to work all night to find her if necessary.

MAYA WISHED she wasn't so in tune to Doug's emotions. He was hurting over their lack of progress in the case, and she was shocked at how badly she wanted to offer comfort.

That unexpected kiss had knocked her off balance. So much so that she'd instinctively kissed him back. It had been so long since she'd been held in a man's arms. She'd foolishly let her attraction to him cloud her senses.

She'd been touched and irked by his apology. It was nice to know he wasn't the type of guy to take advantage of being alone with a woman, but he didn't have to look so appalled by his kissing her either.

Brief as it was, she'd enjoyed their kiss. And deep down, she would have loved nothing more than to kiss him again.

Whatever. She gave herself a mental shake. Slowing the SUV, she turned into the parking lot of the Elk Lodge. As she pulled into the same parking spot she'd used earlier, she thought again about who'd attacked her. A former criminal?

Blaine?

Someone Blaine had paid?

The more she thought about it, the last possibility nagged at her. She couldn't remember if Blaine had friends in Cody, but she made a note to scour his social media to find out.

"Maya?" She belatedly realized she still had the car running.

"I'm fine." Killing the engine, she opened the back hatch and pushed out of the car. "Let's go."

Doug had the laptop case over his shoulder and grabbed the duffel containing Zion's supplies before she could. "Come, Zion," she said, stepping back to close the hatch.

Zion glanced up at her as they headed inside. Maya knew her K9 liked the search game and was bothered when she couldn't find her quarry. "Tomorrow," she said. "We'll play again tomorrow."

Doug unlocked the door, then abruptly stopped. "Get back," he said harshly.

"What's wrong?" She reached for her firearm and glanced up and down the hallway. There was nobody hanging around. "Has someone been here?"

"Oh yeah. The room has been trashed," he said grimly.

Her mouth dropped open in surprise. "You're kidding."

"No. Thankfully, I had my laptop, but they searched my suitcase and generally made a mess of the place." He stepped back so she could see inside.

The place was trashed. No broken items, but the covers had been yanked off the beds, and the contents of his suitcase were strewn on the floor. She'd seen many places that had been searched, and this was exactly what had transpired here. "I don't understand," she said, half to herself. "What were they looking for?"

"No clue." Doug nodded toward the lobby. "I want to talk to that desk clerk. Then we need to find a new place to stay."

Her thoughts whirled as she followed Doug to the front desk. He held his badge up for the clerk. "I'm a federal agent," he said. "Someone has searched our room and my suitcase. You gave someone our key, and I want to know who did this."

The clerk's eyes widened. "I, uh, don't know what you mean..."

"Don't lie to me," Doug barked. "The door isn't broken. You gave the key to someone. Who?"

"Okay, okay!" The clerk looked scared to death. "I know I'm not supposed to give out room keys, but this guy claimed he was Maya Sullivan's brother from the Sullivan ranch and had come to surprise her!"

"Did he give his name?" Maya asked.

"I, uh, don't remember. Charlie? No, Chuck?"

A cold chill snaked down her spine. "Chase? Did he say his name was Chase?"

"Yeah, that's it." The clerk appeared relieved. "Chase Sullivan. His name matched yours, and he looked harmless, so..."

Doug glowered at him. "Where's your manager? I don't care if this guy claimed to be the pope himself, you shouldn't have given him a key to Maya's room!"

"My manager isn't here," the clerk said. And by the way he didn't bother to glance behind him, Maya was pretty sure he was telling the truth. "But please don't talk to him. I don't want to get fired."

"You should be fired," Doug said with exasperation. "Think about what you've done! If Maya had been inside alone, he may have killed her!"

"I'm sorry." The clerk ducked as if expecting Doug to take a swing at him. "I was talking to my girlfriend..."

"Leave him," Maya said, tugging on Doug's arm. "We need to get out of here in case the perp comes back."

Doug grimaced and stepped back. "Fine. I'll grab my suitcase. But I will talk to the manager about this." He turned his attention to the trembling clerk. "And you'll reverse the credit card charge for the room. Now!"

The clerk looked a bit sick as he turned his attention to the computer. Maya waited for him to show her the folio proving her card had been refunded for the room charge while Doug retrieved his luggage.

"You were wrong to give out my room key to a stranger," she said softly. "Agent Bridges is right. That man could have attacked and killed me. Don't ever do that again."

"I—wont." The clerk agreed, his voice subdued. "I just never expected..."

"I know. But crime is everywhere, even here in Cody, Wyoming." She stepped back from the desk as Doug finally returned with his suitcase. "Be thankful no one was hurt by your actions."

The clerk nodded as they turned and headed back outside.

"I can't believe he did that," Doug muttered as he tossed his suitcase and computer bag into the back seat. Then he brought Zion's duffel around to the back.

"I know." She couldn't blame Doug for being angry. Yet she also knew that people out here tended to take situations at face value. If the perp had spoken with confidence, she could almost see why the clerk had been sucked into the ruse. "I don't think he'll make that mistake again."

"He'd better not." Doug waited for her to get Zion settled before opening the door to the passenger seat. Once they were back on the road, he said, "It would be one thing if the perp had pulled a gun, forcing the issue of getting a key. But claiming to be your brother and be handed a key? What is that?"

She headed down Main Street, heading toward the Frontier Hotel. It wasn't as nice as the Elk Lodge, but it would do for now. Her headache intensified, sending her thoughts back to the attack outside the hotel. "I wonder if the man who attacked me is the same guy who pretended to be Chase."

He turned to stare at her. "That's an interesting theory. Maybe he noticed the SUV was gone and used the opportunity to get into the room. But what on earth was he looking for? What did he hope to find?"

"I'm not sure." None of it made any sense. "But obviously, he knew my Sullivan SUV was there and must have figured I had a room there. The Sullivan SUV is likely why he'd used my brother's name to get the key."

The ruse had worked.

Doug was silent for a long moment. "What did he hope to find? It wasn't as if he stayed inside the room, waiting for you so he could strike again."

"That's true." She wasn't sure what to think about this latest twist. "Although he did look through your suitcase. Maybe seeing the male clothing was enough to convince him to bug out of there."

"I hope so." Doug scowled darkly. "He should be running scared. Only the worst kind of coward strikes out at a woman from behind. I'd like nothing more than to get my hands on him."

While she appreciated his protective nature, she didn't really want Doug to be placed in the position of having to fight off her attacker. Zion either. She glanced at her K9 through the rearview mirror. Zion's eyes were closed, and she envied the dog's ability to fall asleep on a dime.

She turned her attention to the road. "That's the Great Frontier Hotel up ahead."

"I remember it from this morning," Doug said with a nod. "It'll work."

It seemed like days ago, rather than just this morning that they'd searched each of the hotels for Emily's scent.

She thought about how Zion had alerted at the Wild Bill Motel. What if the kidnappers had taken Emily to another rental in town? They'd taken the bed linens with them. Maybe they were smart enough to know they'd search the hotels and went with one of John Pickard's rental properties instead.

Yet Cody was still a small enough town that someone may notice a woman being held against her will.

Nothing good came from second-guessing every decision they'd made. She pulled into the parking lot of the Great Frontier with a sigh. She was hungry, tired, and her head hurt.

Doug seemed lost in his thoughts too. She left him to his luggage as she went around to get her dog. Zion's head popped up, instantly awake.

"Out," she said. The dog jumped down from the compartment. She grabbed the duffel, then shut the back.

When they entered the lobby of the Frontier, she recognized the woman behind the counter as one of Justin's classmates. It took her a minute to place the name. "Hi, Skylar," she said. "I didn't realize you worked here."

"Yeah, well, I had to come back to Cody to help care for my mom," Skylar said. "You need a room?"

"Yes, please." When she reached for her credit card, Doug stopped her.

"I'll take care of it," he said. "Do you have connecting rooms? Or a two-bedroom suite?"

Skylar's gaze bounced from her to Doug, then back again. "Yes, we have a two-bedroom suite available," she finally said.

"We'll take it." Doug passed his credit card across the counter. "And I'm trusting you to keep Maya's presence here a secret. She was attacked outside the Elk Lodge just a few hours ago. Do not give our suite number out to anyone, understand? Not even to any of Maya's family members."

"I would never do that," Skylar protested, seeming shocked at the idea. "We don't share our guest names with anyone."

"Yeah, well, some people aren't smart enough to follow that rule," he grumbled. "But thank you."

"Of course." Skylar worked the keyboard, swiped Doug's credit card, then passed two room keys over to them. "The suite is on the first floor, room 1102."

"Thank you." Maya managed a smile. "Take care."

Doug led the way down the hall to their suite. He keyed the room and opened the door. "It's nice," he said, holding the door so she could ease past him.

"I didn't realize you preferred a suite," she said, setting Zion's duffel on the sofa.

"It doesn't matter to me, but you deserve privacy," Doug said. "And I don't want to bother you if I'm up late working."

She nodded, realizing he was just being nice. And trying to reinforce that he wasn't about to jump her bones the minute the lights were out. Not that Zion would allow such a thing. She turned to her dog who was sniffing the room with interest.

"I need to take care of Zion," she said. "You should check out the room service menu."

He nodded and went over to investigate their options. She unpacked Zion's dog dishes, filled one bowl with water, then added two scoops of their preferred dog food to the other. Zion's eyes watched her intently, but she didn't move. She sat tall and straight waiting for Maya to give the signal.

"Go," she said, using a hand gesture to point to the dish. "Go eat."

Zion didn't need to be told twice. She trotted to the food

dishes and began to eat. Zion didn't eat as fast as Trevor's red fox English lab Archie. That dog scarfed so fast they'd had to feed him using a special grooved bowl.

"They have sandwiches and pizza," Doug said. "You decide."

Her chicken sandwich seemed hours away. "Let's go with the pizza," she said. At Doug's smile, she realized that's what he'd wanted to. "I prefer no onions or anchovies."

"Sounds good to me." Doug lifted the phone to place the order. She dropped onto the edge of the sofa. Her headache was making itself known, and she wished she had over-the-counter painkillers to dull the pain.

"Maya, why don't you stretch out to get some sleep?" Doug suggested. "The pizza won't be here for thirty minutes. Long enough for a quick nap."

She opened her eyes to find him standing over her. So close she could have kissed him again. But she didn't. "Thanks, but I need to take care of Zion." She pushed herself to her feet. "Look at how she's sitting by the door. That's her way of telling me she needs to get busy."

"I'll come with you," Doug said as she pulled on her coat.

"No need. Last time, I didn't have Zion. Nobody is going to attack me with her at my side. Besides, I have my gun, and I won't be caught off guard again." She waved a hand at his laptop case. "The best way to find Emily is to figure out who took her in the first place."

Doug hesitated, glanced at Zion, then reluctantly nodded. "Okay."

She pocketed one of the room keys, then opened the door. "Come, Zion."

Zion trotted down the hall retracing their earlier path. The dog knew just where the main doors were located and stood with her nose pressed against the glass as if saying hurry up.

Maya wasn't really worried about her safety, but she pulled her gun from her pocket just in case. She walked with Zion around the corner of the building, finding an area that her dog could use to get busy.

Scanning the area, she narrowed her gaze when she saw someone walking away from the hotel. The guy's shoulders were hunched, making her think he didn't want to be seen. Or recognized.

"Hey! Mister!" She barely took three steps when the guy glanced over his shoulder in her direction. She caught a glimpse of a pale face before he broke into a run.

Oh no, not this time, she thought. "Zion! Get him!" She bolted after the pedestrian, with Zion close at her side. Then her K9 put on a burst of speed, closing the gap.

The perp abruptly veered across the road, jumped into a pickup truck, and started the engine. "Zion, heel!" she sharply commanded as the truck abruptly pulled away from the curb. Zion thankfully spun and returned to Maya's side before the driver could try to run the dog over.

She only caught the first two numbers from the license plate, the prefix being 11, which designated the car as being registered in Park County where Cody was located. The rest of the identifying letters had been covered in snow, not seemingly on purpose the way the mud had been used on the Silverado. But effective all the same.

As she watched the truck's taillights disappear in the darkness, she suddenly wondered if her stalker was somehow related to Doug's missing sister.

And if so, how?

9

When a full five minutes passed without Maya's returning with Zion, Doug abandoned his computer and grabbed his coat. Maybe Zion was taking her sweet time in getting busy, but he couldn't stand waiting. If this guy somehow got past Zion to hurt Maya, he'd never forgive himself.

He headed out of the door and down the hall. Pushing open the lobby doors, he stood for a moment, trying to figure out which way she'd gone.

"Doug?" Maya's voice was surprised. "What are you doing out here? Did you see the truck too?"

"Truck?" He swung to face her. She dropped a baggie into the garbage can, then came toward him. "What truck? What are you talking about?"

She grimaced. "It's probably nothing, but I saw a man who looked a little suspicious. When I called out to him, he took off running. I sent Zion after him, but he managed to reach his truck before she could grab him. I called her back so she wouldn't get hurt, and he drove away. He's local, though, his license plate had the prefix of eleven."

"I don't know what that means," Doug said. He reached for the door. "But let's get inside. From now on, you don't go anywhere alone."

She frowned but crossed the threshold. Together they made their way back to their suite. Doug shot the dead bolt home and then connected the chain lock for added, if somewhat flimsy, protection.

"Wyoming license plates are issued to specific counties, and that county number is the first two digits of the rest of the license plate. In this case, I saw the number eleven, which is the designation for Park County."

"I wondered why so many of the plates started with the same number," Doug said as realization dawned. "I had no idea they were a location designation."

"Rental vehicles can make things confusing," she said. "But basically, the license plate helps identify the county in which the registered owner resides."

"The Silverado plates started with the number eleven," he said thoughtfully. "I guess that means the locals are involved in this mess?"

"Or they know someone local," Maya said. "I should have mentioned the license plate designation sooner."

"No, it's fine. I have the VIN too." He'd sent the information to Ian but had gotten sidetracked with the property owners. The truck was stolen, but he wanted to know more. He entered the Silverado license plate and waited for the information to load. A name popped up on the screen. "Does the name Eric Hine mean anything to you?"

"No, sorry." Maya frowned. "He's the registered owner of the Silverado?"

"Yeah. There's an address here in Cody too." He hesitated, then went to pull the location up on a map. "Do you think the Cody police have been there to question him in person? I know the truck was reported stolen, but I would think they'd verify that claim."

"I'll call and ask." She shrugged out of her coat, then reached for her phone. "If they had found him, though, I'd think they'd let me know."

"True." He used the name to dig deeper. No criminal history, but the Silverado was definitely in Eric's name.

"Hi, this is Maya Sullivan. Has anyone been out to interview Eric Hine about his Silverado?" He glanced over to see Maya frowning as she listened. "Okay, thanks for letting me know."

"What?" he asked, bracing himself for the worst.

"Eric said he loaned the truck to his cousin, Craig Olsen. The officers found Craig at a local tavern. He claimed the truck was stolen right out from under his nose."

"Did they believe him?" Doug asked. "I mean, is this Craig Olsen credible?"

She shrugged. "They sounded as if they believed him, but anything is possible."

"Yeah, I can't help but wonder if Olsen was paid to look the other way so the truck could be stolen." He wanted to speak to this Craig Olsen for himself. "I'll check the property listing, see if his name pops."

"Okay, but it sounds a little too easy," she said. "I can't imagine anyone who takes the sheets off a bed in a dive motel would be foolish enough to leave a trail a blind man could follow. They left the truck, knowing it would be traced back to Eric Hine and Craig Olsen. They wouldn't risk one of them talking."

She was right, it didn't seem likely. The Silverado had been abandoned when it was no longer of any use. He thought about Emily's phone being tucked between the seat cushions, her way of wanting him to know she'd been there.

Glancing at his watch, he realized the pizza would be there in a few minutes. If he had a team at his disposal, he'd send a couple of agents to interview both Eric Hine and Craig Olsen again. But leaving Maya behind to do the task for himself wasn't smart. Her SUV was in the lot, announcing to anyone passing by that she was there.

With a sigh, he scrubbed his hands over his face. He had to work with the resources he had available to him. He'd focus his efforts on digging into his two top suspects using the computer. If he didn't find anything useful, he could head out to interview the two men first thing in the morning.

"Doug? Try not to stress. We'll figure this out," Maya said.

"I know." He dropped his hands and forced a smile. A moment later, there was a knock at the door. He rose, used the peep hole to verify who was out there. Seeing a man standing there with a pizza, he quickly opened the door.

"Thanks," he said, taking the pizza then fishing cash out for a tip.

"Anytime," the room service steward didn't linger.

He set the pizza down, then glanced at Maya. Lines of pain bracketed both sides of her mouth, reminding him she'd been assaulted just a few hours earlier.

And what had he done? Forced her to head out to find an empty cabin in the woods. Kicking himself for being an idiot, he unwrapped the pizza. "Are you hungry?"

"Sort of." Maya tucked a strand of her dark hair behind her ear and stroked Zion.

"How bad is your headache?" he asked.

"Not terrible." She offered a wan smile. "I'll survive."

"I have ibuprofen," he offered. "I tend to carry it with me for those times my shoulder acts up."

"That would be great, thanks." As he dug the bottle from his carry-on suitcase, she crossed over to join him at the table. He gave her the bottle and watched as she downed several tablets. "What happened to your shoulder?"

"I was shot about eighteen months ago." He offered a lopsided smile as he set the computer aside to make more room. "Chasing bad guys, you know how it is."

"I do, but thankfully, I haven't taken a bullet—at least, not yet. My K9 did, though." Her expression turned sad. After a moment, she dropped into a chair. "I'd like to say grace."

"Of course." He sat and bowed his head. To his surprise, she reached over to take his hand.

"Dear Lord Jesus, we thank You for this food we are blessed to eat. We ask You to keep Emily safe in Your loving arms. And we seek Your guidance to find her. Amen."

"Amen." He tightened his grip on her hand for a moment, swallowing hard against the lump in his throat.

Then he pulled himself together. He was touched by Maya's prayer, but he couldn't let himself become sidetracked by her beauty. He waited for her to take a slice of pizza before grabbing one.

They ate in silence for a few moments. "Do you mind if I ask you a personal question?" Maya asked.

"Go for it." He sent her a quick smile. "I'm sure you're wondering about my relationship with my half sister."

"I'm willing to listen to that story, but that wasn't what I wanted to ask you," Maya said, avoiding his gaze. "I would like to know if you're married or engaged or seeing someone."

He flushed. "No! I wouldn't kiss you if I was with someone." He wondered if that was the reason she'd broken off from their embrace. "I was married a long time ago. Gloria and I met in college. We—suffice it to say, we grew apart. Gloria's admiration to my career quickly turned resentful. She wanted someone who had a regular normal job. Not one that caused me to leave the house at odd hours or stay away for extended periods of time."

"I'm sorry to hear things didn't work out," Maya said. "No children?"

"No." He had been a little sad about that, but in hindsight, it was better this way. "Gloria is married to an engineer who works a normal schedule and has two kids. She may have cheated on me in the past, but I don't harbor any hard feelings toward her. She deserves to be happy."

"My ex-husband cheated on me too," she confided. "Blamed my schedule, but I think he was much like Gloria. He wanted someone who would be home every single night the way he was. He works a nine-to-five job at a manufacturing company."

"Those of us with careers in law enforcement have a higher divorce rate than those who don't," he said with a shrug. "It takes a special person to handle that level of stress."

She nodded but didn't say anything more. After finishing two slices of pizza, she rose to her feet. "That was great, but I'm afraid I need to get some rest."

"Of course." He rose to his feet, standing awkwardly beside her. He wanted to pull her into his arms for a hug but offered a smile instead. "Sleep well, Maya."

"Thanks." She held his gaze for a moment, then turned to call her dog. "Come, Zion."

The husky jumped off the sofa and followed Maya into the closest bedroom. Only when the door closed behind her did he sink back down to finish his pizza.

After cleaning up the mess, he went back to work on the

computer. He didn't have Ian Dunlap's skills, but he would do his best.

He needed to find something concrete to go on and prayed it wouldn't take all night.

When Zion nosed her awake, Maya's first realization was that her head didn't hurt very much. The second was that she'd slept all night.

Zion's blue eyes bored into hers. "Okay, girl. I'm coming." She had gone to bed earlier than usual, so she could understand Zion's need to go out. Maya made quick use of the bathroom, then got dressed. She had slept in her underwear in lieu of having pajamas. After taking another moment to tie up her boots, she carefully opened the door.

Zion eased past her as if anxious to go out. She stopped abruptly when she found Doug stretched out on the sofa, asleep.

Why on earth hadn't he used the other bedroom? He must have been down for the count because he didn't stir as she slipped into her coat, then quietly opened the door. Again, Zion was out and trotting down the hall before she could blink.

"Okay, okay." She lengthened her stride. "I'm coming."

Dawn was just beginning to break over the horizon as she stepped outside. Remembering the incident last night made her scan the area for a long moment before following Zion around the corner of the building.

Early winter mornings on the ranch were usually quiet, and she was surprised to find the city wasn't much different. For once, she didn't notice anything amiss.

Zion did her business, then trotted back to her side.

Maya knew the dog loved to play in the snow, but since they'd likely be out searching for Emily again, she didn't take the time now.

"Come, Zion," she said, heading for the door.

When she opened the door to the suite, she found Doug in the act of putting his coat on. "Where are you going?" she asked. "Did you get a lead on Emily?"

"No, I was coming to find you." He looked cranky, and she found his expression strangely cute. "You're not supposed to go outside alone, remember?"

She had forgotten. "I'm fine with Zion."

He scowled as he took his coat off. "I'll make coffee."

"Sounds good to me. Sorry I woke you." She glanced at Zion. "Getting a full night of sleep helped. I feel much better this morning."

"Glad to hear it." He poured water into the four-cup coffeemaker, then leaned against the counter. "I submitted a search warrant request for Nolan's phone and debit card records. Hopefully, we can get those first thing."

"That's progress," she admitted. "What about your other parole? Cortez?"

"He's in jail," Doug admitted. "Which is probably why the parole officer didn't call me back. So we only have Nolan for now, although I went through the other eight names before I conked out. Only one other guy stood out as a strong possibility; his name is Manuel Cartega." When she didn't react to the name, he added, "I discovered his girlfriend was a member of the Robles drug cartel. I found Rosita's death certificate and an article that described how she overdosed on drugs. Not sure why that would be my fault, but he could still be out here seeking revenge by grabbing Emily."

She was impressed. "That sounds promising. Any idea where Manuel is now?"

"No, I tried to keep working, but the screen kept going blurry. I planned to take a thirty-minute nap, but that was four and a half hours ago." He rubbed the back of his neck. "That sofa isn't as comfy as it looks."

"You should have gone to bed. You need your strength if we're going to find Emily," she scolded.

"You know as well as I do we're running out of time." His green gaze turned serious. "I'm worried that we haven't heard from these guys. Makes me think they've taken Emily across state lines. Maybe even across the country."

She knew what he was most afraid of. That these guys would use Emily in some sort of sex-trafficking operation.

"We're going to find her," she said firmly. "All we need is a place to start. Zion's nose hasn't failed me yet."

"Good to know," Doug murmured, turning to pour two mugs of coffee. "Let's order breakfast and draw up a game plan. I'll call my boss. He's an hour ahead of us and will likely be in the office soon. I want him to help get my requested search warrants approved."

"That's step one of your game plan," she teased, sipping her coffee. "Let me guess, you also want to talk to Eric Hine and Craig Olsen."

"Yes. Both men if possible." He glanced at Zion. "If your K9 doesn't alert on Emily's scent, I'll be more inclined to believe they're not involved."

That made sense. "Okay, what's step three?"

"That depends on the search warrants," he admitted. He pulled out his phone. "I'll start making calls to my boss and to the parole officer overseeing Manuel Cartega. If you wouldn't mind ordering breakfast from room service? I'd love steak and eggs over easy with toast and hash brown potatoes."

"No problem." She picked up the menu, then reached for the phone. Doug headed into the bedroom he hadn't used last night to make his calls.

She ordered breakfast, then fed Zion. Her K9 was wide awake and raring to go. "Soon, Zion," she promised. "We'll be playing our game soon."

Zion's curled tail waved back and forth as if in understanding.

Doug was gone for so long she began to wonder if he'd fallen asleep. But then he emerged clean shaven and hair damp from a shower. She grimaced, wishing she'd thought to do the same.

There was a knock at the door. Doug gestured for her and Zion to move to the side, then used the peephole to verify their meals had arrived. He dug out some cash, then opened the door.

"Thanks," he said. The young woman accepted the cash and hurried away. He glanced at her when setting the tray on the table. "I've been in a few situations where the room service clerk was armed and not a room service delivery person at all."

She lifted a brow. "You're not kidding."

"Nope. One guy fired shots through the door, not unlike what happened at Emily's place." He pulled out a chair for her. "I'd love for you to say grace."

"Ah, sure." She was surprised and pleased he'd asked. As she had last night, she took his hand in hers. "Lord Jesus, we thank You for this food You've blessed us with. As we continue to search for Emily, grant us the strength, wisdom, and courage to find her. Amen."

"Amen," he responded without hesitation. "I will gladly take all the strength the Lord will provide."

"Me too." She glanced at Zion who had finished eating and was stretched out between her and Doug, her blue eyes watching them closely. "Zion's ready when we are."

"Great." He dug into his breakfast with enthusiasm. "I know I keep saying this, but I'm grateful for your help."

"Yeah, you can stop now," she teased. "This is what we do. I'd probably be involved even if you hadn't accosted me outside the vet clinic."

He winced. "I didn't accost you," he protested. "But speaking of the clinic, we might want to pick up my SUV at some point. I know you need the extra gear for Zion, but that vehicle of yours announces your presence everywhere we go."

"Maybe later." He had a point about announcing her presence, but her K9's safety was more important. "I can call Chase to get an unlabeled K9 vehicle, but that will take time. The ranch is a solid forty minutes outside of town. Let's focus on these early interviews and go from there."

He hesitated, then nodded. "Okay. But a few hours to get an unmarked vehicle is worth it for you to be safe."

She flushed and hoped he wouldn't notice. "We'll be together, so I'm not worried."

The minute they finished eating, they prepared to hit the road. The hour was still relatively early, not quite eight o'clock in the morning, but she knew Doug didn't care. They'd agreed to head to Craig Olsen's place first as he was the one who allegedly had the Silverado stolen right out from beneath him.

After getting Zion settled in the back, she slid in behind the wheel. Doug had the map of the city up on his laptop.

"The house Craig shares with his wife, Doreen is on the east side of town."

She glanced over at the screen, then nodded. "I need to fill the tank with gas, first. Then we'll head over."

"I'll take care of that for you," Doug said.

She wondered if he'd ever stop trying to pay for her services. It was on the tip of her tongue to mention the inheritance she and her siblings had been granted after her parents' death but stopped herself. Her financial situation wasn't any of his business.

Besides, she couldn't quite forget the flash of greedy anger in Blaine's eyes when he'd realized he wouldn't get a dime of that money. Doug didn't seem to be the type swayed by wealth, but she didn't even want to go there.

What was the point anyway? As soon as they found Emily, he'd buy a one-way ticket out of Cody to head home.

And she wasn't leaving the ranch under any circumstances.

When Doug finished filling her tank, she drove through the quiet streets of the city. Residents were beginning to stir now, heading off to work or school. She and Chase had encouraged Kendra to finish her last year of high school in person, but Kendra had asked to complete her courses online instead.

Maya had been so happy Kendra had become close to Emily these past few weeks. She couldn't imagine how Kendra would respond to losing a close friend and made a silent vow to do everything possible to find Doug's sister.

"It's the third house on the right," Doug said. "I see smoke coming from the chimney, so someone is up."

"A lot of folks have wood-burning stoves," she said, pulling into the driveway. "They burn all night."

Doug nodded. "I know, but there's a faint light in the

kitchen." He glanced at her. "I'll take the lead on asking questions. You give Zion the search command. If she alerts anywhere near the property, I'll push my way inside."

"Without a warrant?" When he simply shrugged, she sighed. "Okay. Let's do it."

She released Zion from the rear hatch. Knowing they wouldn't be outside for long, she didn't bother with the booties. "Are you ready?" she asked with excitement. "Are you ready to work?"

Zion's tail wagged, and the dog lifted her snout to the air. She gave her a sip of water, then offered Emily's socks for another sniff. Zion looked up at her as if to say, *Yes, I remember*. "Search. Search for Emily."

Her K9 sniffed the air, then lowered her nose to the ground. Maya closed the rear hatch and watched as Zion worked. Doug went up to the door and knocked.

A tired-looking woman answered the door. "Who are you?"

"Federal Agent Doug Bridges." He flashed his badge. "I need to speak to Craig Olsen."

"Craig!" The woman's tired expression turned angry. "Craig! The federal government is here!"

"What in the . . ." The guy stopped abruptly when he saw Maya and Zion.

"Are you Craig Olsen?" Doug asked. "You were in possession of a Silverado truck that was stolen?"

"Ah, yeah." To Maya's eye, Craig looked very nervous. "Why? Is that a federal crime now?"

Zion was doing her zigzag pattern around the front yard, making her way up to the front door. Craig stared at the dog sniffing his clothing as if frozen with fear.

Then Zion turned in a circle, sat directly in front of the partially open doorway, and looked over at Maya.

Zion had alerted on Emily's scent!

10

Upon seeing Zion's alert on his sister's scent, Doug wrenched the screen door the rest of the way open and pushed his way inside. Craig was wearing a stained sweatshirt and drawstring pants. There was no sign of a weapon.

"Hey," Craig protested as Doug shouldered past him. "You can't barge in here!"

"Where is she?" He scanned the room. The woman who'd opened the door and who he assumed was Craig's wife, Doreen, stood off to the side holding a baby. "Where's Emily?"

"Who?" Craig's confusion seemed real, but Doug wasn't buying his innocent act, especially as it pertained to the stolen Silverado.

"Sit down. You too, ma'am," he said to Doreen. "I'm searching for a kidnapped woman named Emily Sanders, and the K9 alerted on her scent."

Craig's jaw dropped. "That's impossible! I don't know anything about a kidnapped woman."

"I assure you it's not impossible at all," Maya said calmly

from the door. She'd entered the house, too, with Zion at her side. The dog sniffed the air with interest. She met Doug's gaze. When he nodded, she leaned forward. "Search! Search for Emily."

Zion lowered her nose to the floor and moved eagerly through the room. She sniffed all around even going down the hallway and checking each doorway, before returning to the main living space. The K9 then veered abruptly toward where Craig stood off to the side of the kitchen. She sniffed his feet and his hands, then sat and turned toward Maya with an expectant look.

"You were with Emily," Doug accused, crossing the room toward him. "And you're going to tell me where she is."

"I d-don't know what you're talking about," Craig stammered. "That dog is crazy. I don't know anything about a missing woman."

"Craig?" Doreen glared at him. "If you're lying..."

"I'm not," Craig protested hotly. "I didn't take anyone."

"I never said you kidnapped her, just that you were with her," Doug pointed out. Then he reached out, grabbed Craig's arm, and roughly spun him toward the wall. "Fine. You want to do this the hard way? I'm done playing around. Craig Olsen, you're under arrest for obstruction of justice and aiding and abetting a kidnapping." He ruthlessly wrenched both of Craig's wrists behind his back. "You have the right to remain silent. Anything you say can and will be used against you in a court of law."

"What did you do, Craig?" Doreen demanded as the baby in her arms began to wail. "What did you do?"

"Wait! Stop! I didn't do anything," Craig protested.

"Zion says you know more than you're telling," Maya said, giving Doug an exasperated look, likely annoyed with his heavy-handed approach to the situation. Too bad. He needed answers. "If you cooperate with us, I'm sure Agent Bridges will let you go."

Doug gritted his teeth for a moment, wrestling his anger under control. "That's right. Cooperation is your only way out of this. Where is she? I want to know who has Emily and where they're holding her."

Craig's gaze darted between his wife and Maya, then landed on Zion who was staring at him intently. Sensing the gig was up, he reluctantly nodded. "Okay. Okay, I was in the truck with a woman, but that's all. They dropped me at the bar and took off. I swear that's all I know!"

"Who?" Doug demanded, tightening his grip on Olsen's wrists. "Who took her?"

"Ow, you're hurting me!" When Doug didn't loosen his grip, Craig added, "I only know one of the guys who had her, Steve Beldon. He offered me five hundred bucks to give him the keys to the Silverado and to wait to report it stolen."

"You idiot!" Doreen screamed. "You told me you got a new job!"

"Yeah, well, I didn't," Craig shot back. "Get off my back, woman. I gave you half the money, didn't I?"

"And what did you do with the other half?" Doreen demanded. "Drank it at the Crooked Wheel, didn't you?"

Her mentioning the bar where the shooting took place was interesting. He loosened his grip just enough to convince Craig to keep talking. "Okay, you mentioned Steve Beldon. Who else was involved?"

"I, uh, just the Mexican dude, along with the woman." Craig glanced at him. "She wasn't hurt or anything. But the Mexican pretty much pushed me by force out of the truck when we reached the bar. He said something about needing to hurry because some guy was hurt."

That surprised him. "What do you mean hurt?"

"How should I know?" Craig's tone was whiny. "I didn't ask questions. I took the cash and got out of the truck. They took off down Main Street."

"Which way down Main Street?" Doug pressed. "East or west?"

"West," Craig answered without hesitation. "I watched for a moment before going into the Crooked Wheel. I think they were going to Wild Bill's, but I can't say for sure." He darted another anxious look toward his wife, who was glaring at him with such ferocity Doug almost felt sorry for the guy.

Almost.

He turned to glance at Maya, ignoring the angry interchange between Doreen and Craig Olsen. "Do you think it's possible the injured guy at the motel had been Emily's patient? That they kidnapped her to help take care of his injuries?"

Maya slowly nodded. "Could be that his wounds opened and bled all over the place. That would explain why they took the bed linens and towels. They wouldn't want anyone to believe a crime had taken place there. And they wouldn't want the DNA tested either."

Doug wasn't sure if he was going down this path because it was more palatable than thinking about the possibility of Emily being used for sex trafficking or if they were onto to something. He released Craig's wrists and spun the man back toward him. "Where can I find Steve Beldon?"

"He has a place on the north side of town." Craig rubbed his wrists. "I swear I don't know anything more. I didn't think they were gonna hurt her or anything."

Doug grabbed Olsen's sweatshirt and pushed him back against the wall. "You witnessed a kidnapping and didn't call the authorities. That makes you an accomplice. So help me, if Emily is hurt in any way, I'll be back. I will prosecute you to the fullest extent of the law. Do you understand?"

Doreen began to sob. "No, please. You can't arrest him! What am I gonna do if you arrest him?" The baby in her arms wailed louder now as if picking up on the stress vibrating through the room.

He didn't bother to look at her, his gaze fixated on Olsen. "Do you have contact information for Beldon? A phone number? What car does he drive?"

"Yeah, I have a number." Craig dug in the pocket of his drawstring pants and retrieved his cell. He swiped the screen one-handed, then scrolled with his thumb. "Here. He drives an old blue Ford pickup truck, but it's not reliable and doesn't have an extended cab back seat. That's why they wanted the Silverado."

"What sort of criminal activity is Beldon involved in?" He quickly memorized the number on Olsen's screen. When Craig didn't answer right away, he narrowed his gaze. "I know he's involved with something. Drugs, most likely. Am I right?"

Olsen darted a look toward his wife, then shrugged. "Yeah, he buys and sells drugs. But I'm not into that scene. I just needed the cash, that's all."

He wasn't sure he believed him about not being involved in drug trafficking, but that didn't matter. He didn't have time to arrest Olsen. Taking a step back, he glanced again toward Maya. "Anything else you can think of?"

A smile tugged at the corner of her mouth. "No, I think you've covered it."

"Thanks for your cooperation," Doug finally said. "But if I learn you called ahead to warn Beldon, I'll be back to toss your sorry butt in jail. Understand?"

Olsen swallowed hard. "Yeah, I got it." He glanced at his wife, then added, "I won't call him."

"Good." Doug turned toward Maya, then he had an idea. "Wait, on second thought, you should call Beldon. Right now."

"I should?" Craig looked uncertain.

"Call him, then hand me the phone." Doug stepped closer. "Hurry!"

With shaking fingers, Craig placed the call. "He didn't answer. The call went to voice mail."

He hesitated, then took Craig's phone. "Does your wife have a phone?"

"Yeah, why?" Olsen asked.

"Because I'm going to borrow yours. You'll get it back by the end of the day." Doug pocketed the device. "Thanks again for your cooperation."

"Wait, you can't do that," Olsen protested.

"By the end of the day," he rashly promised. "Let's go, Maya."

Maya didn't look happy as she opened the door, letting Zion out first, then stepping out into the cold. Doug followed her back to the SUV. She tossed Zion the bunny. "Good girl, Zion! Good girl!"

"I can't believe she was able to pick up Emily's scent from him," he said in admiration while texting Ian for Beldon's address. Ten seconds later, Ian texted him back. "Got the address."

Maya nodded and turned toward Zion. "Hand."

Zion trotted over to give the bunny back. Maya tucked it away and opened the hatch. "Probably because Olsen hadn't showered. Otherwise, we may not have been successful."

He nodded in understanding. Maybe God was helping

them. Moments later, they were back on the road, heading north to Beldon's place.

"I wonder if Beldon has other properties," Doug muttered as he brought the laptop computer to life. "Maybe a hunting cabin?"

Maya shrugged. "I doubt a low-level drug dealer is interested in hunting and fishing." She gave him the stink eye. "You don't really have the right to steal his phone."

"I need it to keep tabs on Beldon." He couldn't bring himself to feel bad about what he'd done. "They have a phone at the house, and he's not working. They'll be fine for a few hours. Besides, this Beldon may not be a low-level drug dealer. He may be more connected with the cartels than we realize."

"Maybe." Maya's tone was noncommittal. As if she were still upset with him.

Squashing the flash of guilt, he brought up the property listing Ian had sent earlier to make sure he hadn't missed a second property for the guy.

He hadn't.

"The name Steve Beldon sounds familiar," Maya said while navigating the city streets. "I wonder if I arrested him at some point."

He closed the laptop and glanced at her. "Do you think he's your assailant?"

"Not sure." She stopped at the next intersection, then turned right. "It's interesting that he's here in Cody if I did arrest him back when I was a cop in Cheyenne. I'll dig into his arrest records soon."

The drug connection nagged at him too. The hospital was small enough that he knew the kidnappers may have taken Emily only because she was a nurse and not his half sister. Yet he still had two men who had a list of guys who had been released from prison one of whom could be seeking the opportunity to settle a score.

"It's that second house from the end of the street," Maya said. "Doesn't look as if anyone is home."

He swallowed hard and found himself praying Beldon was home. They could issue a BOLO for his vehicle, but he wanted to find Emily now. Before things could take a turn for the worse.

Maya pulled into the driveway but kept the engine running. He reached for his door handle. "I'll go first and check things out. Stay inside where it's warm."

She shot him another exasperated look and pushed out of her side without killing the engine. "I'll back you up. These guys are armed and dangerous."

Clearly, she wasn't going to sit back and let him take all the risks. Torn between annoyance and admiration, he gave her a curt nod. The house appeared empty, but he intended to make sure. "Take the left side, I'll go right."

"Meet you around back," she agreed, then turned to slink along the edge of the house. He took the right side, peering into the first window that wasn't covered by blinds or drapes.

Nothing. He moved to the next, and the next. Most of the windows were covered, making it difficult to see inside, but those windows that weren't revealed no sign of life. Beldon could be sleeping, but a quick look in the garage revealed it was empty too.

He and Maya met around back. "I didn't see anyone," she said.

"Yeah, I didn't either, but some windows were covered." He considered their options. "Can you see if Zion alerts on Emily's scent?"

"Sure." They hurried around to the front of the house.

Doug continued peering through windows and checking doors as Maya and Zion searched. He wasn't surprised when they didn't find any evidence of Emily having been there.

Both doors were locked, but the one in the back was flimsy. He used a credit card, wiggling it between the doorjamb and lock, working the handle to push the latch out of the way.

He got it open. Sweeping a quick glance around the backyard to make sure no one was watching, he went inside.

The house reeked of garbage, as if Beldon hadn't taken it out for a while. He poked his head into each of the bedrooms, only to verify they were empty.

He went back outside to join Maya and Zion. "I managed to get inside, but the place is empty."

She arched a brow at that, but simply said, "Sorry to say Emily hasn't been here."

"I figured." He sighed, frustrated with knowing they'd reached another dead end.

And Emily had been gone for twenty-five hours and counting.

MAYA WAS surprised at how Doug had crossed the line, first with pushing his way into Olsen's house, then breaking in here at Steve Beldon's. Obviously, he was desperate to find Emily, but she'd have pegged him for being a rule follower.

The way she'd been while on the job. Being involved in search and rescue operations gave her more leeway.

"I know what you're thinking," Doug said, once they were back inside the SUV. "I know I'm operating outside the legal boundaries of the law, but we're running out of time. Emily has been gone for twenty-five hours." The clock on her dash read eight thirty in the morning. "I don't have time to work the system."

"Your actions could result in the bad guys getting off," she said. "That's all I care about."

"I know, and I'll figure that out when the time comes." He stared off into the distance. "I need those search warrants. And I want to add Beldon's phone too." He held up Olsen's device. "I'll keep trying, maybe Beldon will return Olsen's call."

"Maybe. We'll probably have better luck with the search warrants." He was so upset at finding nothing at Beldon's home that it was difficult to blame him for cutting corners. "I think we should head back to the hotel."

"Okay." He sounded resigned, and she was surprised at how much she wanted to offer him some comfort.

"Hey, we know the last time Emily was seen, she wasn't hurt," she said. "And it appears they took her to help their injured perp. That's good information, Doug."

"I really want to believe they haven't hurt Emily," he admitted. "And while the information is helpful, we need more."

"I understand." She grimaced, and added, "It would be good to find Beldon's current location. It stands to reason Emily will still be with him and the other two men."

Doug glanced at her, then began working his phone. "Maybe Ian can ping his phone."

She headed back to the Great Frontier Hotel as he made the calls. He finished just as she pulled into the parking lot. "Okay, the search warrant for Cartega's phone and credit card records has come through. Ian is trying to ping Beldon's phone." He sighed. "It's a start."

"We're going to find her," she said reassuringly. "We're on the right track."

"I hope so." He offered a lopsided smile, then pushed out of the SUV. She killed the engine and released the back hatch. Zion bounded out as if anxious to be on the move.

"Get busy," she said, taking advantage of the time outside. "Get busy, Zion."

Her dog whirled and trotted to the side of the hotel. After Maya cleaned up the mess, she turned to Doug who had waited, despite the cold. She glanced up at the swirling dark clouds and knew more snow was on the way.

If they had to go on another search, they'd likely need snowshoes. They had several sets back at the ranch, but she decided to wait to see if they got another lead.

Knowing Doug, he'd rather buy them than waste time driving back and forth to the ranch. Maybe he had more money in his bank accounts than she did.

Nah, that wasn't likely. But he didn't appear to be hurting for cash either.

He held the door open for her and Zion. "Those clouds look ominous."

"I agree." She glanced at him, noting he'd brought his laptop inside. "Let's hope we get something off the search warrant info."

"I scanned it briefly but didn't see anything that appears to indicate Cartega is here in the Wyoming area." He scowled. "He could be using cash, though, too. I need you to make sure I'm not missing something. Hopefully, they'll fast-track the warrant for Beldon's records."

She nodded and waited for him to unlock the room. Since she'd already fed Zion, she decided not to head back out for the dog's duffle bag.

"Here, see what you think." Doug set the computer on the table, made sure the document was up on the screen, then stepped back. "The area code is 307, correct?"

"Yes, that covers the entire state, so that won't help narrow the call down to Cody or Greybull." She shrugged out of her coat and took the seat. There were dozens upon dozens of phone calls. She frowned and glanced at him. "Cartega worked for the cartel?"

"Yeah. And his girlfriend died of a drug overdose." He shook his head. "Seeing the volume of calls makes me think he's right back in the game."

"I agree." She kept scrolling until she found what she was looking for. "Doug? Here's a number with 307 as the area code."

He leaned over her shoulder to see the screen. "Really? That call was placed two days ago. And there are several more calls after that." He turned to look at her. "He's here. Manuel Cartega is in Wyoming."

"Looks that way to me." She could feel his excitement. "What's Beldon's phone number?" When he read off the digits, she entered them into the search bar.

No match.

"Maybe they're using disposable phones," Doug said. "Any of those purchased here would have the same area code, right?"

"Most likely." She scanned the Wyoming numbers but didn't recognize any of them. She brought up a search engine and typed in the Crooked Wheel. Their website and phone number came up on the screen. When she put that number in the search bar, there was a match.

"Doug, look." She gestured to the screen. "Cartega called the Crooked Wheel two days ago too."

He nodded. "We can go over and ask around about Cartega and Beldon. But even if they were there at some point, that doesn't help us find them now. The place didn't look big enough to house extra rooms where someone could hide. Besides, I don't think they'd have stayed in a place open to the public."

"I agree, the bar was likely an initial meeting spot. Maybe if we can find something more recent, we'll have somewhere to look." She went back to the list, trying to ignore the way Doug continued reading over her shoulder. He was too close for comfort.

Oddly, Zion didn't seem to mind. Her previous K9 partner Ranger had barely tolerated her ex-husband, Blaine. He hadn't growled or snapped his teeth, but more often than not, Ranger would put himself between the two of them.

She missed Ranger. He'd been in his last year of service when he'd been killed. After wrestling her grief, she'd pulled herself together. Having already decided to move on from the police department, she adopted Zion as a puppy, moved back to the ranch, and began training her. She was pleased with how well Zion had adapted to her new role as a search and rescue K9.

Maya was confident Zion could find Emily, if they could narrow their search field to a reasonable location.

"Hold on," Doug said, when she was about to move onto the next screen. "That number there belongs to the Wild Bill Motel."

"And that call was also made two days ago." She glanced over at him. "Maybe they went straight from the hospital to Wild Bill's."

"When did the injury happen?" Doug asked. "I'm trying to put a timeline together in my mind. It appears as if Cartega met someone, maybe Beldon, at the Crooked Wheel. Maybe from there, they did some drug business. Is that when the mystery guy was injured? But if he was knifed or shot at, the police would have been notified by the ED doc, right? Those are automatic reports to law enforcement."

"They are, yes." She could see the scenario he described in her mind. "Maybe they did go to the hospital, but then left. They may have holed up at Wild Bill's, then went back to grab Emily."

"Yeah." He looked thoughtful. "I wonder what made them move from Wild Bill's."

"The gunman fired at us from the Crooked Wheel," she reminded him. "He may have heard about a federal agent asking about his sister. That would be a big deal around here since we so rarely interact with the feds."

He straightened and began to pace. "We're close, but I still can't figure out where to start searching for Emily."

She glanced toward the window. The dark clouds were heavy with moisture. She had a bad feeling that they weren't looking at a minor two-inch snowfall this time. The wind picked up, and she could imagine a full-blown blizzard letting loose.

They needed something to go on, and soon. Before they were stuck inside.

Her thoughts returned to Beldon. Why was his name familiar? She quickly checked his criminal record, but nothing popped. She hadn't arrested him.

Remembering her theory that her assailant was somehow connected to this, she went to Blaine's social media page. It didn't appear as if he'd posted anything for the past two years, which was odd. The good news was that he hadn't bothered to block her on the site. Probably because he knew she didn't post anything about her personal life there. Most cops didn't broadcast their home-life for every criminal to see.

She went to his list of friends and scrolled through the names until she found it.

Steve Beldon.

Beldon was here in Cody and a friend of her ex-husband. She sat back in her chair, stunned. Was Beldon her attacker? Had he struck her over the head because she was helping Doug Bridges find his sister?

The timeline didn't make sense for that, as she'd first noticed him popping up behind her two weeks ago.

No, the more she thought about it, the more likely it was that Blaine had sent him after her to even the score.

11

"What is it?" Doug hunkered down beside Maya's chair. She looked as if someone had smacked her in the face. "Did you find something?"

"Yeah." She drew in a deep breath. "Appears my ex is friends with Steve Beldon. Which means he knows Beldon is involved in criminal activity and may have hired him to attack me."

He frowned. "Could be Beldon is a thug for hire and that your ex reached out to him. But maybe that idiot is here in Cody. Your ex could have attacked you."

"Blaine didn't hit me over the head," she said. "I would have recognized him, even with only a quick glance. Back when I first noticed someone lurking nearby, I checked with Blaine's employer. The manager of the plant claimed he was working. Which makes sense now that I know he likely hired Beldon to do his dirty work."

"I don't know about that, Maya. In my experience, men with a personal grudge would rather take care of the issue for themselves rather than hire it out."

"You don't know Blaine," she scoffed. "He's not very motivated. Plus, he knows I'm a cop and would likely recognize him. Hiring someone to hurt me on his behalf is right up his alley."

He nodded. She knew her ex-husband the best, and he trusted her judgment. "Why would he want you to be attacked? Was he upset about the divorce?"

"He was upset about not getting any money," she said. Then she seemed to catch herself. "Never mind, just trust me that Blaine likely hired Beldon to attack me. And if that is the case, Beldon isn't hiding out with the other bad guys." Her eyes widened. "Unless they're close enough that he can drive back and forth."

As much as he was curious about what money her ex thought he was entitled to, he focused on Emily. "He was in town when he attacked you outside the Elk Lodge. And he must have been the one to pretend to be your brother to get access to the room."

"Yeah, Blaine must have mentioned my family. The assault was about three thirty in the afternoon. We left an hour later to check out that cabin."

"Maybe Beldon was told to stay in town to keep an eye on us." He shrugged. "Maybe attacking you was done for two reasons. To keep you from doing any searches with Zion and to give Blaine some satisfaction."

"I hope we find him," she said with a scowl. "He deserves to be arrested."

"I'm on board with that plan," he said, striving to keep his tone light. They were making progress, but the deep sense of urgency wouldn't leave him alone. Between the ticking clock and the impending storm, he sensed they didn't have much time.

What would happen once Emily's services were no longer needed? Would they simply leave her behind?

Or kill her to keep her from going to the police?

He tried not to dwell on the worst-case scenario, but it wasn't easy. He was keenly aware of the ruthlessness of the cartel.

When his phone rang, he gratefully reached for it. "Hey, Ian, please tell me something good."

"I finally got into the system and was able to identify the last cell tower that pinged Beldon's phone. It's in Cody, all right. Unfortunately, that city is so small the tower covers the entire area. I can't get down to anything more specific than that."

His heart sank. "Okay, thanks for trying. What about the search warrant? Has that come through?"

"We're waiting to hear from the judge," Ian said. "The minute it's granted, I'll run those reports."

He tried to think of another angle to pursue but came up empty. "Okay, keep me in the loop."

"Will do." Ian ended the call.

He turned toward Maya. "May I use the computer?" He quickly pulled up Steve Beldon in the DMV database. "Would you call the Cody PD to ask for a BOLO to be issued for this truck?" He turned the screen so she could see the license plate that started with the Park County 11 designation. "You seem to have a better rapport with them."

"Of course." He listened as she made the call. When that was finished, he began to pace. There had to be another angle to work. But what?

"The Crooked Wheel," he said, spinning around to face her. "We need to ask around about Beldon. Maybe someone saw him last night. He may have gone there after searching through our hotel room."

Maya nodded. "Okay, it can't hurt to try." She glanced toward the window. He followed her gaze. It wasn't snowing. Yet.

"As long as we're heading out, we should think about picking up a few pairs of snowshoes," Maya added. She lifted her chin toward the window. "Those clouds are going to bust a gut sooner or later. If we happen to get a lead on Emily's location, we need to be prepared to work in less-than-ideal conditions."

"That's fine." He was more than willing to learn how to use snowshoes, but the idea of dragging Maya and Zion into danger did not sit well with him. A glance at his watch indicated it was going on nine forty-five. Emily had been missing for twenty-six hours now and he still had no idea where to find her. "We'll stop to buy the snowshoes first since the hour is still rather early. What time does the Crooked Wheel open anyway?"

"Hang on." Maya worked her phone. "They open at nine. But you know it's not likely the same crowd that was there last night will be there bright and early this morning. When I worked in Cheyenne, it was the third-shift crowd that gravitated to the bars early in the morning."

He wondered if Emily had ever gone there with some coworkers after work. Not that it mattered. He understood Maya was pointing out the limitations in his plan to interview the locals at the Crooked Wheel, but he couldn't bear the thought of waiting until later that night to do the job.

He wanted Emily to have been found safely by then.

"Doug?" Maya said, interrupting his thoughts.

"I know, different crowd," he agreed. "But we need to try."

Maya reached for her coat. "There's a large store that sells sporting goods; they'll have snowshoes." She held his gaze for a moment. "Or we can drive to the Sullivan ranch. I have plenty there we can borrow."

"Too far," he said, shaking his head. In truth, he'd have loved to see the ranch. But not while Emily was missing. "I don't care about the cost. I'll pay for the snowshoes."

"I figured as much." Her smile was wry. "But just wanted to let you know there were options. Come, Zion."

The dog lifted her head, stretched, then padded toward Maya. He shrugged into his coat, then grabbed the laptop, shoving it into the case. He hadn't bothered to take his suitcase out of the SUV. "I think we should keep the room another day," he said as they headed down the hall to the lobby. "Emily will need a place to rest and recover once we find her."

Maya nodded in agreement.

He waited as she stopped at the desk to make the arrangements, then they headed outside. The thick layer of clouds swirled over the city. They hung so low they obscured his view of the snowcapped Bighorn Mountains.

Where are you, Emily? He stared out the window as Maya drove to the sporting goods store. Was his sister being held somewhere in the city? Or out in the snowy countryside?

His gut leaned toward the latter, but he didn't want to overlook the obvious.

Less than ten minutes later, Maya pulled up to the sporting goods store. The place was huge, and he realized it was likely the only store in the city. Maya didn't hesitate to bring Zion inside. It seemed that the locals didn't mind having dogs trailing after their owners.

Or maybe it was just that Maya and her family were well known in the region.

"This way," Maya said, gesturing for him to follow. He eyed the gun counter with interest, seeing rifles and shotguns along with a wide variety of handguns available for sale.

In some ways, Wyoming was the epitome of the wild, wild west.

He found Maya inspecting rows of rectangle-shaped snowshoes. He'd heard of them and knew some people used them for fun. But he eyed them warily now, wondering how they worked.

"We'll probably want the package," Maya was saying. When she noticed his confusion, she added, "Snowshoes and poles. If you're not used to walking in them, you'll want the poles to help keep you steady."

They looked too much like the cane his grandmother had used after her hip surgery, but he held his tongue. "Whatever you think is best."

"Okay." She picked out a pair of men's-sized snowshoes for him and a smaller size for herself. She had gotten the package, too, which made him feel better.

The cost was higher than he'd anticipated, but he paid without complaint. If they helped him reach Emily, then it was well worth the price.

When they were back outside, Maya gestured toward a park. "Let's give them a try so you can see how they work."

"Now? We need to get to the Crooked Wheel."

She arched a brow. "Better to learn how to walk in them now than waiting until after we get a lead on Emily."

He chafed at the delay but nodded. She was right. If they found a lead on Emily's whereabouts, he needed to be able to move without difficulty. "Fine. Let's do this."

"Don't sound so excited," she chided. "It's not hard, but it's also not as easy as it looks."

He followed her to the park. She explained how they worked, the base of the shoe providing a way to distribute a person's body weight over a wide area to prevent him from sinking into the snow.

She secured the straps, then handed him the poles. "Have you ever gone cross-country skiing? It's similar to that, but without the gliding motion."

"No, sorry." His ex-wife had a point about his life being all work and very little play. "But I have gone downhill skiing."

"This is different." She took a minute to put her own snowshoes on. Zion pranced around in the snow as if she loved this weather. "Okay, follow me."

Maya walked across the snow with short strides. She was right, it wasn't as easy as it looked. But soon he was able to find the groove.

"People do this for fun, huh?" he asked as they paused to rest. Despite the cold, he was working up a sweat.

"Out here, we use them out of necessity, not entertainment. But yes, some do this as a form of working out."

He grunted. Give him an indoor gym any day. He stayed in shape because of his job, but this was something only a die-hard snow lover would do. Leaning on his pole, he turned to see how far they'd come. Then winced when he realized they'd barely gone a hundred yards.

"Okay, we can head back now," Maya said. "Turning can be a challenge, don't cut it too close or you'll trip yourself up."

Her warning came too late. He was face down in the snow before he could blink. The sound of Maya's laughter made him groan.

"Sorry, I shouldn't laugh." She bent and retrieved his pole so he could stand.

"It's fine." He couldn't blame her for seeing the humor of the situation. He managed to rise to his feet by leaning heavily on the pole. The one he'd almost refused to use. "Thanks."

He realized Maya was staring past him, and he quickly glanced over his shoulder.

"Look! A truck!" Maya snowshoed past him with a speed and agility he envied. "That might be Beldon's truck!"

Sure enough, he caught a glimpse of a blue Ford pickup. He carefully turned around to follow her. Clearly, she'd been right about his need to practice. She looked as if she was flying over the snow with Zion leaping gracefully beside her. The dog reached the truck first, sniffing with interest.

Then to his surprise, the dog turned to stare at Maya. The husky didn't alert the way she usually did upon finding Emily's scent, but the dog seemed to be telling them something was amiss.

His gut tightened as he approached. There was frost on the windows, making him think the vehicle had been there for a while. At least a couple of hours.

Maybe even all night.

He headed around to the driver's side, while Maya peered through the narrow gap of the passenger-side window.

He swallowed hard when he noticed something dark was pressed up against the driver's side window. A man's head? With a sick feeling, he tugged on the driver's door handle. The vehicle wasn't locked, and the door creaked in protest as if the joints had rusted while it was sitting there as he wrenched it open.

Steve Beldon's body fell out. A dark bullet hole marred the right side of his temple.

They had hit another dead end.

Literally.

"Stay back," Maya warned, knowing Doug was smart enough not to mess with evidence but wary of his new penchant for crossing the line to get what he wanted. "I'll call it in."

Doug ignored her, bending down to examine the body. "Hard to tell if it's murder or suicide."

"We have a dead body on the north side of Lion's Park," she told the Cody dispatcher. "Victim is believed to be Steve Beldon, and he has suffered a gunshot wound to his right temple."

"A gunshot wound?" the dispatcher echoed in shock.

"Yes. Unclear if the injury is self-inflicted or the result of foul play." Knowing the role Beldon played in the kidnapping case, she was leaning toward homicide. But this wasn't her case. "Please hurry."

"Both units are on the way," the dispatcher assured her.

"Thanks." She stuffed the phone back into her pocket and quickly drew on her gloves. The wail of sirens was reassuring.

"I don't like this," Doug said, rising to a standing position. He held her gaze for a moment. "It feels like they're tying off loose ends."

"I don't like it either." She sighed, knowing he was concerned that Emily would be another loose end. She didn't know what to say to make him feel better. All they could do was keep searching.

She glanced down at Zion who stared up at her with those bright-blue eyes. Her K9 wasn't trained to find cadavers like Alexis's dog, Denali, but the husky had known something was wrong.

Maya bent and stroked her gloved hand over Zion's fur. "Good girl. You knew he was in there, didn't you? Good girl."

Doug grimaced. "I noticed how she reacted to the truck. Her nose is amazing. It's so cold I didn't catch the scent of decay until I opened the door."

"I'm sure he was out here most of the night. Likely froze solid from the way he dropped to the ground like that." She glanced around the area. "No cameras around here either." Her eyes widened. "Hey, what are you doing?"

"Looking for his phone." Doug patted Beldon's pockets, then stood to peer into the truck. "I don't see it. The killer likely took it with him."

"You need to let the crime scene techs do their thing," she said with annoyance. "They'll search for clues as to what happened."

"We're running out of time." Doug's green eyes flared with a mixture of anger and frustration. Not with her, she realized, but the situation. "Emily could be the next one left in a car with a bullet wound to the head. We need to find her before they decide she's outlived her usefulness."

"I know that. I do." She blew out a breath, a puff of steam forming in the air. "As soon as the squad arrives, we'll head to the Crooked Wheel."

He closed his eyes for a moment, then nodded. "Thanks."

The wail of sirens could be heard well before the two officers arrived. She wasn't surprised to see they were the same two that had been on duty yesterday.

"Maya, Agent Bridges." Burt Jones nodded in greeting. "How did you happen to stumble into this crime scene?"

"Thanks for coming." Maya shared Doug's impatience but couldn't bring herself to shortcut the investigation. "I called earlier about issuing a BOLO for Steve Beldon's truck.

He is—or rather was—a person of interest in the kidnapping case." She gestured at the truck. "We were practicing using snowshoes when I spotted it. Zion indicated there was something strange inside, and when Doug opened the driver's side door, Beldon fell out."

"Who gave you the information regarding Beldon's involvement?" Sergeant Tom Howell demanded. "I was going to follow up with you about that."

"We were able to convince Craig Olsen to come clean," Doug said. "He was paid five hundred bucks to claim the Silverado was stolen. He saw Emily but claimed she wasn't hurt. He identified one of the men as Steve Beldon. The other was a Hispanic we believe could be Manuel Cartega, who was recently released from jail back in Wisconsin. Cartega has known ties to the Mexican drug cartel."

Maya could see the news had stunned both officers. Sergeant Howell's face turned red, but Jones said, "You really think members of a Mexican drug cartel are way out here?"

"Yes." Doug shrugged. "I have Cartega's cell phone records. He made several calls to numbers with a 307 area code."

The two officers glanced from her to Doug, then down at Beldon's dead body. "Guess we should consider this a homicide," Howell said grimly.

"Yes, you should." Doug sighed. "Look, do you have a detective or someone that does these investigations? I'm happy to send the phone records over. But my sister is still missing, so if you don't mind, we need to go."

"I'll be in touch," Maya added, trying to soften Doug's hard edges. "We want to find the person responsible as much as you do."

"We work with the state Criminal Investigation Unit,"

Jones said. "If you send me the data, I can make sure it gets up the chain of command."

"Okay." Doug took a moment to send the information he'd gotten via the search warrant to Jones's email. Then he remembered Olsen's phone and pulled it from his pocket. "This needs to get back to Craig Olsen. If you find anything more, I'd appreciate a call." When Sergeant Howell looked as if he might argue, Doug hastily added, "I promise I will do the same. We called you for this, and if I find anything else related to Emily's disappearance, I'll fill you in on that too."

"Yeah, okay." Jones took Doug's offer at face value, although Maya sensed Howell wasn't convinced even though he accepted Olsen's phone without saying a word.

She appreciated Doug's efforts to smooth things over with the local cops, and added, "We'll keep you in the loop."

"Thanks again to both of you." Doug turned to her. "Ready?"

She nodded. "Come, Zion." The husky bounded to her side and kept pace as they snowshoed back across the park where they'd left her SUV.

Doug's expression was grim as he removed the straps around his boots. "Thanks for the lesson. I won't slow you down if we need to use them."

"I know you won't." As she said the words snowflakes fell from the sky. Lightly at first, but soon they filled the air. "And yeah, we're going to need them."

She started the car and opened the rear hatch for Zion. Doug placed his snowshoes and poles in the back passenger seat, then came over to grab hers.

"I was hoping the snow would hold off," he said as they settled in the front seat. Snowflakes coated his eyelashes, and she had to stop herself from reaching over to brush them away.

"Me too." She sat letting the warmth from the heated seats sink deep. Then she put the car in gear and pulled away from the curb. "I hope we find someone at the Crooked Wheel that will talk."

"They'll talk," Doug said with a dark frown. "I'm not in the mood for anything less than full cooperation."

She thought about Steve's death as she drove to the Crooked Wheel. Maybe she was wrong about Steve being hired by Blaine to attack her. For all his faults, she couldn't imagine Blaine committing cold-blooded murder.

Granted, she hadn't seen him in five years. Could her ex-husband have changed that much? Being a cheater was one thing.

Murder was on a whole different level.

She made a mental note to double-check that Blaine was still working at the manufacturing plant in Cheyenne. If he was, she could deal with his hired thug later.

If he wasn't? Her stomach rolled. Could Blaine really be involved in something like this? Kidnapping and murder?

She thrust the possibility away as she pulled into the Crooked Wheel parking lot. It was only yesterday that she and Zion had searched for gold and found the shell casing.

Yet it seemed as if she'd known Doug for weeks rather than hours. Weird, because she hadn't experienced that phenomenon with any of her previous cases.

She was letting her attraction for him cloud her senses. The guy was skating on the edge, fear for his sister's safety overriding his obligation to play by the rules.

"I'll take the lead," he said gruffly, before opening his door and climbing out.

"Yeah, yeah." She shot him a narrow glare. "Don't push it, Doug."

He grimaced, gave a terse nod, and slammed his door shut. She retrieved Zion and followed him up to the front door. He held it open, so she stepped inside with Zion.

It took a minute for her eyes to adjust to the dim interior. Snow coated the windows, eliminating some of the natural light.

Doug headed straight for the bar where two older men sat in front of two glasses of beer. It was barely ten forty, and their mugs were half full. She hung back, listening as Doug addressed them.

"Excuse me, which of you knows Steve Beldon?" He asked as if their knowledge was a foregone conclusion.

"Who wants to know?" the balder of the two asked.

Doug flipped open his badge. "Agent Bridges, I'm investigating a kidnapping and a murder. If you don't want to cooperate, I'll toss you in jail and find someone who will. I'm running out of time. So start talking."

She took a step forward. This was his idea of not pushing it?

Then to her surprise, the guy with dirty gray hair said, "Yeah, we know him. But he ain't here. Left last night. Said he had to meet an old friend."

An old friend? The knot in her stomach tightened painfully. Blaine? Battling a wave of nausea, she pulled out her phone and went back to her earlier social media search. This time she wasn't looking for her ex-husband's friends, but for his mother's maiden name.

Swanson. Tanya Swanson. Blaine had once mentioned his grandfather had a cabin outside of Cody. He'd gone there as a kid.

And that could very well be where Emily was being held now.

12

Doug was losing his patience. Badly. He needed these guys to tell him everything they knew. And somehow, he felt certain they were holding back.

"Who was his old friend?" he pressed.

"I dunno." The guy with the gray greasy hair didn't even look at him.

"Doug." Maya yanked on his arm, hard enough to pull him off balance. "We need to go. I think I know where she is."

"You do?" He stared at her in surprise. "Where?"

"Come with me." She tugged on his arm again, and this time he didn't hesitate to turn his back on the two older men. They were halfway to the door when she added, "I think Steve's old friend is Blaine. My ex-husband."

He frowned. "I don't understand. I thought your ex was in Cheyenne."

"I thought so too." She paused before heading out into the bitter cold. "When I first noticed someone behind me two weeks ago, I called the manufacturing plant to verify he was working. They said he was." She held his gaze. "Blaine was very bitter about money. If he was offered easy money in exchange for doing something illegal, I think he'd take it. I searched his social media and discovered Steve Beldon is listed as one of his friends. From there, I remembered that Blaine's grandfather has a hunting cabin about halfway between Cody and Greybull."

A wave of anticipation swept over him. "What's his grandfather's name?"

"Last name is Swanson. I think his first name was Herbert, and his wife was Edith. Blaine's mother is Tanya." She waved a hand toward the door. "Let's go. We can get the location off the property report your tech guy ran for us."

He pushed open the front door and was hit in the face by a swirling mass of snow that seemed to have doubled in volume during the ten minutes they were inside. The flakes were small and pelted his skin like tiny ice picks.

Ducking his head, he pushed forward creating a path for Maya who huddled behind him. He cut a path to the SUV and brushed the snow off the windows while she remotely started the engine and opened the rear hatch for Zion.

Once they were settled inside, he pulled out his laptop computer to find the address for the property. When he found it under the name of Herbert Swanson, he glanced at her. "Have you been to this cabin?"

"No." She kept her eyes on the road as visibility was getting worse by the second. The vehicle handled the snowy roads fairly well via the four-wheel drive, but he couldn't help but wonder how it would do if they ended up hit with six inches or more. "We may have to wait until the storm passes."

He shook his head. "Please don't ask me to do that. If you can get me to the area, I'll go in on foot. You can stay in the vehicle and call for backup."

She sighed. "And what happens if you get lost? It's easy to get confused in the middle of a blizzard."

"I know. I tend to have a pretty good sense of direction and can always use my phone as a compass." He spoke with a confidence he didn't really feel. He would rather not head out by himself, but waiting for the storm to pass wasn't an option.

Maya didn't say anything, just continued driving east. He looked again at the map of where the Swanson property was located. It was south of the highway rather than north, so not likely the source of the smoke he'd seen yesterday.

He'd coerced Maya into going on a wild-goose chase yesterday. Time that would have been better spent working the case. Yet investigations could be tricky. They may not have uncovered the connection between Steve Beldon and Blaine any faster. He knew better than most that investigations could be broken open by the smallest thing.

Like interviewing two old men where one mentioned how Steve had headed out to meet an old friend.

"How did you connect Steve meeting an old buddy to your ex-husband?" he asked.

"I'm pretty sure Steve and Blaine went to high school together." She spared him a quick look. "I discovered they're still friends on social media too. I never met Steve, but Blaine mentioned his football pals several times, referring to one of his wide receivers as Stevie. Blaine was a quarterback and went on to play football in college on a partial scholarship. That's where we met. During our sophomore year, he blew out his knee, had surgery, and dropped out of school. Once his knee healed, he decided to work Trocar Metals manufacturing company."

He considered that for a moment. "You really think

Blaine went from being a former high school football star to being capable of murder?"

"I don't want to believe that." Her voice was full of regret as she continued heading east. Their pace was slow but steady, and considering the snowfall, he couldn't ask for anything more. "But it wouldn't surprise me if he'd changed for the worst. Blaine always wanted more. More money, more stuff, more . . ." Her voice trailed off.

"Greed can take over a person's life," he said.

"Yeah." She was silent for a long moment. "I have to wonder if Blaine asked Stevie to follow me, maybe trying to scare me into coming back to him."

He arched a brow. "He does know you're a former cop, right? I don't see you running to any man even if you were afraid."

She let out a harsh laugh. "Funny how you know me after being together for twenty-four hours better than he does, and we were married for four years. Yes. Even if I was freaked out about being tailed, I would never go back to Blaine. For many reasons, but mostly because he cheated and blamed my job as a cop for his lack of morality and commitment."

"Jerk," he said, inwardly reeling from her comment about how well they'd gotten to know each other in such a short time frame. He'd felt the same way about her. Their kiss was still far too fresh in his mind. He forced himself to focus on the situation, not his growing feelings for Maya. "You're better off without him."

She nodded. The SUV slid sideways on the slick road. Maya was able to regain control of the vehicle without difficulty. The wind caused snowdrifts, and he felt guilty all over again about asking Maya to do this.

Consulting the laptop, he estimated they had another

five miles to go. He tried to scan the landscape out his passenger window but couldn't see much beyond the snow-covered trees.

As much as he hated to admit it, getting lost was a distinct possibility.

"There's still time to change your mind about this," Maya said. Her ability to read him was uncanny. "It's not likely they'll leave the cabin in this weather."

"I know you're right about that, but them being stuck on the property works in my favor. What if they take off the minute the snow stops? I'll have missed my chance to rescue Emily." He shook his head. "I need to try."

She didn't respond. He hated disappointing her, but he didn't see that he had another option. When she slowed the SUV and edged toward the side of the road, he tensed.

This was it.

Once he headed out into the blizzard to find the cabin, there would be no turning back.

"See that narrow opening between the trees?" Maya asked. "I believe that's a gravel road that will lead toward the driveway."

He frowned. "It doesn't look as if anyone has driven a vehicle down there recently."

"Yeah, I noticed that." She sighed. "Maybe there's another way into the property. Or maybe they drove to a location where they picked up snow machines." She turned in her seat to face him. "Or maybe we're wrong about Blaine, and Emily isn't here. I wish you would consider waiting until morning."

"If there's a cabin in the area, I'll find it." He glanced at the narrow opening again, telling himself that following the road couldn't be that difficult. "If Emily isn't there, I'll build a fire and hang out until the storm passes."

"Fine." She pushed the gearshift into park. "We'll come with you."

"No!" His tone came out more vehement than he'd intended. "Please, Maya, I don't want to risk you and Zion. I need you to head back into Cody to arrange for backup."

"Here's a better idea." She jutted her chin at a stubborn angle. "We go together with Zion and make sure Emily is there. Once we verify that, we both return to the SUV and call for backup."

"I refuse to risk your life," he repeated. "Or Zion's. Give me time to find the cabin. If it appears occupied, I'll text you to call for backup."

"We're coming, end of story." She waved her hand impatiently. "Sitting here and arguing is a useless waste of time. The snowstorm is growing worse by the minute."

He held her gaze. "Please reconsider staying here."

"Nope." She pushed open her driver's side door, letting in a gust of snowflakes. "Let's move."

As he slid out of the car into the blustery wind, he sent up a silent prayer begging God to watch over them.

If his decision to head out in this storm hurt Maya or Zion, he'd never forgive himself.

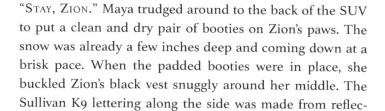

"STAY, ZION." Maya trudged around to the back of the SUV to put a clean and dry pair of booties on Zion's paws. The snow was already a few inches deep and coming down at a brisk pace. When the padded booties were in place, she buckled Zion's black vest snuggly around her middle. The Sullivan K9 lettering along the side was made from reflective material that would catch the light even from a distance.

She had more faith in Zion's nose and the dog's ability to

track Emily than in her ability to stay on course. Between her compass that was thankfully not dependent on her phone and Zion's nose, she was confident they'd be fine.

Barring any issues like freezing to death or falling down a ravine.

Once Zion was set, she and Doug strapped on their snowshoes. She dug an extra face mask out of the compartment underneath the crated area for him. He looked grateful for the additional protection.

"We're going to let Zion take the lead," she said, her voice muffled by the face covering. "She'll get us to the cabin."

"Okay." His green eyes reflected a sincere gratitude. "I appreciate you doing this."

As if she could walk away and leave him to venture out alone? Yeah, no matter what he'd thought, that was never a viable option. She pulled two protein snack bars from her pocket and offered him one. "We'll need fuel to get through this."

"You think of everything, don't you?" he asked as he unwrapped the bar and took a bite.

"Yep." She ate the protein bar then turned her attention to Zion, setting the stage for their upcoming mission. The husky was always willing to play, but she liked to set the tone, revving the dog up with excitement. "Are you ready, girl? Are you?" She poured a little water into a dish and offered it to her partner. Then she switched to offering the bag containing Emily's gloves and socks. Zion sniffed them only for a moment before looking up at her with pale-blue eyes as if anticipating the command. Maya suspected Emily's scent was engraved in her dog's memory. "Are you ready to work? Let's search! Search for Emily!"

The husky trotted a few feet away, lifting her snout to the

air. Maya closed the back hatch, locked the SUV, then snowshoed across the surface of the newly fallen snow.

She shouldn't have been surprised how quickly Doug had adapted to the snowshoes. He used them with an athletic grace her ex didn't share, despite his partial football scholarship. She wrestled with guilt over the possibility that Blaine was working with criminals who'd kidnapped Emily.

For money. With him, it was always about the money.

Zion bounded through the snow with excitement, giving her hope they were on the right track.

Catching up to Doug, she consulted her compass. She tipped her head down to keep the snow from getting in her eyes. "According to the map and my coordinates, we'll need to head southeast for at least a mile." She glanced up at him. "If this is the dirt or gravel road leading to the driveway, I doubt it's a straight shot to the cabin. Most roads aren't. Wandering Creek runs along the side of the property, so that is something we need to take into consideration. The water will be frozen and covered with snow, making it difficult to see."

"That makes sense. I appreciate the information." He used his poles to help propel him forward. "Zion is on the move."

Her K9 loved the snow. Huskies were bred for this type of weather. Yet Maya noted the way Zion sniffed the area with interest. Her K9 kept her nose in the air rather than trying to scent along the ground. Falling snow inhibited scent tracking to a certain extent, but once they found the cabin, Maya was confident Zion would be able to zero in on Emily's scent.

If the young woman was or had been there.

Following Zion's lead, they headed across the stretch of land that led to the narrow opening between the pine trees.

The heavily laden evergreens significantly reduced the impact of the wind. Not only did the temperature feel warmer, but she could see their surroundings much easier. Despite how the hour was edging toward noon, the overcast sky and swirling snow made it seem much later.

They snowshoed down between the trees at a brisk pace. As she'd anticipated, the road curved first to the right, then to the left.

The blanket of snow brought an eerie silence to the area. Other than the wind, there were no other discernible sounds. Wildlife hunkered down in this weather, burrowing deep into the snow and thick brush to stay warm.

When Doug paused at the next curve, her pulse kicked up. She caught up to him with two strides. "What is it?"

He pulled the face mask down and sniffed the air. "Am I imagining it, or is that the scent of burning wood?"

She frowned and pulled her face mask aside as well. After a long moment, she shook her head. "Sorry, but I don't smell anything."

"Wishful thinking," he muttered, replacing the mask. With a muffled voice, he said, "We're not going to see rising smoke through all this snow, are we?"

"Nope." As they resumed their trek forward, she kept an eye on Zion who trotted from one side of the open area to the other. Her K9's ears were pricked forward, her expression alert. "We're only human. Zion will be able to scent burning wood from a fire, so let's trust her to lead the way."

"I totally trust Zion to keep us on the right track." From the way the corners of his eyes crinkled, she assumed he was smiling.

Despite the frigid temps and the snow that was covering them now from head to foot, she caught his sense of purpose. As if just knowing they might be close to finding Emily was propelling him forward.

As they followed the bend in the road, she could only pray she wasn't leading him down the wrong path. They'd come here based on her gut instincts. And the connection between Blaine and Stevie that couldn't be ignored.

But if she was wrong? She swallowed hard and tried not to think about that as she leaned on her poles for balance.

Her K9 darted out of sight. "Zion!" she called as loud as she could through the face mask. "Zion, come!"

It took a few seconds for the dog to come galloping back. The snow settled on Zion's fur, making her look bigger than normal. Zion stood for a moment, gave herself a shake to get rid of some of the snow, then wheeled and ran off again.

Zion's footprints in the snow were the only ones marring the glistening surface before them. She and Doug were leaving tracks, but glancing back over her shoulder, she could see the snow was already filling the marks.

Hopefully, there would be enough of a path for the local and state police to follow once they verified Emily's location and called for backup.

There was still no sign of a cabin, and when they left the shelter of the trees, the snow obscured her vision. She squinted to keep an eye on Zion, catching glimpses of her K9's vest through the snow.

Doug suddenly lurched sideways, leaning heavily on his left pole to keep himself from falling headfirst into the snow. She cautiously made a circle around him to see what had happened.

His left pole was way down in the snow, indicating there was a dip in the ground below the layer of snow. She could just barely see the indentation and couldn't blame him for missing it.

"You okay?" she asked, as he struggled to regain his balance.

"Yeah." He pulled his pole free and gingerly took a few steps forward and to the right to keep away from another hidden hazard. "At least I didn't fall."

"Good job." She was impressed with his ability to stay upright. "How are your ankles? No injuries?"

"Wrenched the left one a bit, but I'm good." He blinked the snow from his eyes. "Let's keep going."

She nodded and turned to look for Zion. The dog was a few yards ahead, staring at them as if to say, *What's taking so long?* "We're coming," she called. The dog turned and continued forward.

It took a solid twenty minutes for them to go one mile. And even then, she almost missed the path heading to the left.

Tire tracks. They were full of snow, but the two tracks were clearly visible. Narrowing her gaze, she realized they had come from the opposite direction. Her earlier theory of the kidnappers taking an alternate way to reach the cabin appeared to be true.

"We're getting close," Doug said. "The cabin can't be too much farther."

"Don't bet on it," she warned, as they followed the faint tire marks. Zion was still well ahead of them. Since the K9 didn't alert, she figured the dog must have caught some other scent.

They trekked for another twenty yards. That's when she smelled it too.

Burning wood.

"I think I see the side of the cabin," Doug said, his voice low and muffled. "It's about seventy yards ahead."

"Zion must see it too." She nodded toward her K9. "See

how she runs ahead, then comes back to stare at me? She wants us to hurry."

"We can't just rush forward," Doug protested. "We need to figure out where the windows are so we can avoid being seen."

"I doubt they're expecting anyone to be out in the storm." She didn't mention just how crazy they were for being there in the first place. "But we do need to proceed with caution. Assume they're armed and dangerous."

He nodded and gestured toward a cluster of trees to their right. She understood and carefully turned to head toward them. "Zion, come!" She didn't want the dog to get close enough to attract attention.

Five minutes later, they reached the shelter of the trees. Her fingers and toes were cold, but the rest of her body wasn't too bad. The exertion of using the snowshoes helped keep her torso warm.

The wood-burning scent was stronger here, and she could see the dark structure of the cabin up ahead. Snow blanketed the roof, and while she still couldn't really see any smoke rising from the cabin, there was a bare patch without snow around the chimney.

Someone was there. Not only could she smell the smoke, but the faint tire tracks led to a large garage. She caught a glimpse of an orange glow from a fire through the large picture window overlooking the front yard.

"I think we should head to the back of the cabin," Doug whispered.

"I agree." She nodded at the garage. "If they brought Emily in there, maybe Zion will alert."

His green eyes flared with hope. "Let's try."

She glanced down at Zion. "Search!" she said softly but with unmistakable enthusiasm. "Search for Emily!"

Her partner shot out from the trees, the snow covering her coat helping her blend into the environment. The dog ran straight toward the garage, sniffing along the ground, then lifting her nose to the edge of the garage door.

Then the K9 sat and turned to stare at Maya.

"She alerted," Doug said with anticipation. "Emily is here!"

"She was here and may still be here," she corrected. "Let's see if we can get to a window to check for sure."

Doug stared at her. "You think they may have killed her?"

"I didn't say that, but we need to get a visual." She gestured toward the cabin. "They could have brought Emily here, then left again before the snow started to fall."

"I doubt that, but I'm all for getting closer." Doug eased out from behind the trees and carefully headed toward the garage. His clothes were covered in snow, too, as were hers, so maybe nobody would notice.

Unless they decided to look outside and catch a glimpse of their snowshoe tracks.

She followed Doug to the garage, relieved when she reached the structure without incident. The building blocked the wind, but when they went around to the back, the wind slammed them in the face.

Lowering her head and using all her strength on the poles to push forward, she followed Doug to the back of the cabin. There were smaller windows along the side of the house closest to the garage, and she wondered if they were bedrooms.

Zion stayed close to her side. Maya hadn't rewarded the K9 yet, but she would once they had a positive ID.

She couldn't bear the thought that they'd come all this way during a blizzard for nothing.

Doug reached the windows first. He stayed to the side, peering cautiously around the corner. She went to the next window to do the same thing.

No blinds or curtains covered the windows, which was a blessing. Yet there weren't lights on inside either. At first glance, she couldn't see anything. Not even furniture, a bed, or dresser.

Then her vision adapted to the dim light, and she could see the form of someone lying on the bed. Not a woman, she noted, but a man.

Not Blaine, this guy had dark hair, and Blaine was blond. Maybe the injured bad guy? From what they'd learned from Craig Olsen, Emily had been taken because one of them was hurt.

She turned to look at Doug. He shrugged as if to say he wasn't sure what to make of the guy, either, when she caught movement from inside.

A woman came into the room carrying a large bowl of water.

Emily! She saw Doug react, too, and knew their search was over. She needed to call for backup. It would take the local police time to get there, but they could head back to the SUV and wait for them to arrive.

Digging her phone from the inside pocket of her coat, she brought up the screen to dial 911 when she saw the words *No Service*.

They were out of cell range, or the tower signal was obliterated by the storm. She lifted her gaze to Doug and shook her head. He grimaced and dug his phone out, but it was no use. He quickly stuck it back into his pocket. His phone didn't have service either.

They were on their own.

13

Not having cell service was a problem, but Doug wasn't going to let that stop him from getting inside that cabin. He was armed and so was Maya. More importantly, they had the element of surprise.

Granted, he couldn't feel his fingers or toes, so shooting accurately may be problematic. But they were too close to head back now.

Turning his attention back to the bedroom window, he tried to get Emily's attention. Unfortunately, it was rather dark inside the room, and she was intensely focused on her patient. From what he could see, Emily had towels and a damp cloth. She appeared to be cleaning the upper right portion of the guy's chest. A wound of some sort, he guessed. He couldn't hear anything and sensed he wouldn't be able to distract Emily until she was finished.

She still wore her scrubs from work, which was slightly reassuring. There were no obvious signs that she'd been sexually assaulted. The way she was caring for the guy on the bed indicated her main purpose was to provide nursing services.

Until her expertise was no longer needed. After that, he knew all bets were off. Steve Beldon had been brutally murdered in a scene that had been staged to look like a suicide.

He had no illusions these men wouldn't hesitate to take Emily out of the picture in much the same way.

Doug took a quick moment to thank God for watching over his half sister. Then he turned toward Maya. "We need to know how many perps are inside."

She nodded and gestured to the side of the house. He nearly groaned when he realized there were two large patio doors, extending from floor to ceiling. No way of getting past them undetected. "Keep an eye on Emily," she whispered. "I'll see who else is inside."

"You stay here." He didn't want Maya in any more danger than she already was. While grateful to have found Emily, he was the one who needed to take the risks moving forward. She'd done more than her fair share.

Without giving her time to argue, he ducked low and shuffled his way down along the side of the house. An orange glow of light flickered through the patio doors.

The living room.

Chances were high that the bad guys were sitting close to the fire while Emily tended to their wounded cohort in crime. He drew a deep breath, then edged closer to peek into the room.

Two men with their backs to the doors were sitting with their booted feet propped up on the coffee table, looking as if they didn't have a care in the world. Clearly, they were not expecting to be found. He was glad he'd pushed the issue of checking on them now rather than waiting until the following day.

The guy closest to him was Hispanic, exactly as the Wild

Bill clerk had described. Possibly Manuel Cartega, although he couldn't say with certainty without seeing his face. Cartega had a handgun tucked into his waistband.

The other perp had dirty-blond hair. Presumably Blaine, but in truth, it didn't matter one way or the other. He was with Cartega while Emily was in the other room. That made the blond man guilty by association. He backed away, assuming Blaine was armed as well. With at least a handgun, but maybe a rifle too.

This was Blaine's grandparents' hunting cabin after all.

Knowing there could be a third man, he tried to figure out how to check the other side of the house. Going past the patio doors wasn't an option. He'd have a better chance going past the large window facing the front.

It took him several minutes to get in place. When he reached the bay window, he crouched low so that his head wouldn't clear the window frame and duckwalked—no easy feat while wearing snowshoes—until he reached the other side.

Another bedroom, but it was empty. Where was the kitchen? He returned to the front door and the bay window. He crept up to the house and looked inside. From this angle, he could see the Hispanic man's profile. The guy looked like Cartega, although the facial hair made him look older than Doug remembered. He still couldn't see the blond guy very well, but behind the two men, he could make out a small kitchen.

There was a pan on the stove and some open cans of what was likely soup on the counter. Other than signs that someone had eaten, the kitchen appeared to be empty. It wouldn't surprise him if these yahoos forced Emily to cook for them as well as providing nursing care to the injured man.

Battling a stab of anger, he turned to continue checking the rest of the house. As he moved from window to window, thankful not to see anyone else inside, he formulated a plan of attack.

The only way to get Emily out of there safely was to create a diversion. He needed to draw at least one of the perps outside. With either Blaine or Cartega out of commission, he stood a better chance of overpowering the second man.

Unless the wounded perp grabbed Emily to use her as a human shield. He winced, trying not to go down that path.

Heading back to the SUV wasn't an option. It would take too long, and he was growing colder by the minute. He was sure Maya was freezing too.

No, they were going to get this done. Right here, right now.

He turned to make his way back to where he'd left Maya watching over Emily. He had to duck below the bay window again, then went back to meet with Maya who was still outside the injured man's bedroom. He was about to say something when he heard a thumping sound.

He froze, his heart lodged in his throat. Had one of the perps seen him? Were they right now heading out to investigate?

Maya cocked her head and pointed at the bedroom window. He frowned, not getting it, until he edged closer to look inside.

Now he understood. The thumping sound was the man who'd been in the bed. Emily had her arm around the guy's waist, helping him walk presumably to the bathroom, but he hadn't gotten far. He was slumped against the wall, Emily holding him upright with all her strength. After a long minute, the man pushed away from the wall and continued shuffling back toward the bed.

He nodded at Maya, then gestured for her to come away from the window. Zion was sticking close to Maya's side as if sensing the danger. He knew the K9 was very much in tune to Maya's emotions. The dog had alerted him to Maya's injury last evening.

Maya hesitated, tilting her head to the bedroom window, but he gestured again. There was no point in standing there any longer. Emily was too preoccupied with her patient, and they had to move quickly.

"I only saw two men," he said when they were back behind the garage. "A Hispanic who is likely Cartega and a blond guy I assume is Blaine. They're both armed, and I'm sure there are other weapons inside."

"Blaine is blond, so I'm sure he's involved in this up to his eyeballs." Maya glanced toward the bedroom window, then back at him. "If we can get Emily's attention, she can help us with the diversion."

"No. I'd rather have her stay in the bedroom well out of the line of fire. We need a distraction." He glanced around the area. With the thickening layer of snow covering everything in sight, he searched for something he could use as a diversion. Looking for a rock to throw was laughable. Maybe a tree branch?

"I think we should break into the garage," Maya whispered. "I'm sure we'll find something inside to use as a diversion."

She was so smart he wanted to kiss her. He settled for nodding and taking the lead to head around the garage to the side door they'd passed earlier. The door was locked, but he jabbed his elbow against the window to break the glass. Thankfully, the tinkling sound was muffled by the snow.

Moments later, they were inside. The interior was dark, ambient light only coming from the broken window in the door. He nearly tripped over his snowshoes, they weren't helpful for walking on concrete, and bumped into the SUV. Leaning against the car, he removed his gloves so he could unbuckle the snowshoes.

A small light flicked on, and he was surprised to see Maya had a flashlight. Well, he wasn't really surprised as she seemed to think of everything. More so than he had. He could take lessons from this woman and still be two steps behind when it came to dealing with an emergency.

"Thanks," he said, wishing the garage was heated. When his boots were free from the snowshoes, he knelt beside Maya to take care of removing hers. His fingers were cold and stiff, so he blew on them to warm them.

They would be in deep trouble if he was unable to fire his weapon.

"What's the plan?" She knelt to care for her dog. Zion shook her body, sending snow and water everywhere. Maya blinked, wiped at her eyes, then examined her K9's paws. The booties were covered with snow, making them look twice as large. He felt bad for putting her and the dog in harm's way.

The sooner he could take care of these kidnappers, the better.

He glanced around the interior of the garage. The SUV took up one bay, and a snow machine sat in the other. He knew they hadn't brought Emily here on the sled, so that one must belong to Blaine's grandfather.

He sighed, weighing his options. "My plan is rather rudimentary. I'll slam something at the front of the house, drawing the two men to the front door. At least one of them will step outside where I can take care of him. You'll need to cover the back patio doors in case one of them tries to rabbit out that way." He noticed a wall with various tools hanging off the wall and gestured toward them. "One of those should do the trick."

"Take care of him how?" She'd removed her face mask so he could see her frowning. "You can't just shoot first and ask questions later."

He could, but that wouldn't be legal or ethical. Seeing Emily in person as she cared for the injured man had dulled his anger to a certain point. Although he still didn't know for sure what she'd suffered during the past thirty-plus hours or so. "I hope to catch him off guard long enough to disarm him. When I make my move, you'll need to attract the second guy's attention."

Her gaze was skeptical. "Maybe I should try to draw Blaine out. He knows me and may cooperate."

"No." His tone was hard and unyielding. "You don't know the man Blaine is now. Cartega is ruthless. He could easily kill you without blinking an eye." The more he thought about his plan, the worse it sounded. "I'm hoping Cartega will be the one to come out and investigate my diversion. But if your ex takes the lead, I want you to make some noise to draw attention to the back, then get far away from the house." *Out of gun range*, he thought grimly.

She shot him an exasperated glance, then stood. Zion stood beside her like a silent sentinel. The dog rarely barked, a rather curious trait for a dog. Yet maybe that had been part of Zion's training.

Crossing to the wall of tools, he considered his options. He picked up a hammer, considered the torque wrench, then noticed a jack stand lying on the floor. Spying the crowbar next to it, he picked that up. It was lighter than the torque wrench, making it easier to swing as a weapon. He glanced at Maya. "What would you like? The crowbar or the torque wrench?"

Her brows lifted. "Crowbar."

"Here you go." He handed it to her, then placed the hammer in his pocket. His goal wasn't to break the window, but to make thumping sounds that would draw the men out of the house.

He turned to face Maya. "Are you ready?"

Her gaze was solemn as she nodded. "Yes. We only fire in self-defense, and the goal is to keep Emily safe."

"Agree." He moved closer. "And I want you and Zion to be safe, too, okay? Let me do the hard work."

"I'm not helpless," she said, annoyed. "I know how to protect myself."

Logically, he knew she was right. But he couldn't bear the thought of her being hurt or worse. He reached for her hand, tugged her close, and kissed her. Her lips were cool but instantly warmed beneath his. For a long moment, they held each other close. Zion bumped her nose against him, making him smile.

Then he broke off from their kiss and took a step back. As much as he'd rather spend time with Maya, it was time to get to work.

But once Emily was safe, he wanted to see Maya again. Just the two of them. Alone.

Well, maybe with Zion too. But without the threat of danger looming over them.

He pulled his face mask up over his nose and mouth, drew his gloves on, and headed toward the garage door. He purposefully left the snowshoes behind. The trek to the front door would be difficult, but from there, he'd need to be agile. To move quickly in order to take whichever perp came to the front door.

This was it. As he stepped back out into the blizzard, he prayed.

Please Lord Jesus, keep Maya, Zion and Emily safe in Your care!

∽

SHAKEN by Doug's potent kiss—she'd momentarily forgotten they were in the garage of Blaine's grandparents' cabin—Maya pulled her protective gear into place.

"Come, Zion." She held the crowbar in one hand and followed him out into the snow. The wind was stronger now, whistling between the trees. The tracks they'd made earlier were full now, leaving just the slightest indentations behind.

Walking in the deep snow without the snowshoes wasn't easy, her foot sank to mid-shin with every step, yet she understood the need to leave them behind. Hopefully, they would be inside the cabin sooner rather than later.

Zion stayed at her side as she made her way around to the rear patio doors. She took a quick moment to peer into the bedroom window. Thankfully, Emily was still inside the room with her patient. They appeared to be talking, and she wondered if Emily was trying to convince the injured man to let her go.

Hopefully, Emily would stay put once Doug put his plan into action. She had her weapon but couldn't use it while wearing gloves. Doug had the same issue. The armed perps had the advantage of being inside a warm dwelling.

The thought of Blaine and Cartega pulling their weapon and firing at her and Doug was sobering. This plan could easily go sideways. She glanced at her K9. Zion's fluffy coat was covered with snow again, so she felt certain they wouldn't see or aim at her dog.

At least Cartega wouldn't. Blaine knew her well enough to realize that hurting her dog was the worst thing he could do. She considered sending Zion back to the garage, then decided it was better to have her partner nearby. Besides, as well trained as Zion was, she knew the husky would come running to protect her once things started happening.

And that may distract her from her mission. No, it was better to keep the dog close.

Maya pressed her back up against the side of the house and peered around the edge. The glow of the fire made her yearn to get closer; she was so cold her body was shivering. That was a good sign, but it wouldn't take long for hypothermia to set in.

She saw Blaine and Cartega relaxing in their respective chairs, boots up on the coffee table. Apparently, they hadn't moved in the time she and Doug had gone to the garage and back. She held the crowbar ready in case one of them decided to come out the back.

For several long seconds, nothing happened. Then she heard the distinctive thump as Doug slammed the hammer against the wall.

Both men straightened in their seats, turning to face the front window. When Maya realized she was holding her breath, she forced herself to breathe. After another long moment, the two men relaxed, apparently assuming the thudding noise was snow falling off the roof or taking down a tree branch.

Then Doug hit the side of the house again. Despite the wind and swirling snow, she was able to hear the sound. Again, the two men glanced at each other, then Cartega pulled his feet off the table and stood.

She could see Blaine telling him something, likely attempting to convince him the sound was nothing to worry about. A reluctant smile tugged at the corner of her mouth at how well Doug's plan was working. She steeled herself to take action, watching as Cartega went to the picture window overlooking the front yard.

Come on, open the door, she thought. *Open the door and step outside.*

He didn't. After peering through the window for ten seconds, he turned to say something to Blaine.

Now what? Should she make noise back here? Waiting was torture, and she tried to think like Doug.

Thump! Thump! Thump!

The three bangs came close together, sounding as if he were kicking his foot against the front door.

Her breath caught in her throat as Cartega pulled his weapon from his waistband and reached for the door handle. She lifted her crowbar, wrapping her gloved hands around the base, waiting for the right time.

As if viewing a movie in slow motion, she watched as Cartega pulled the door open and took a step forward leading with his weapon. When she caught a blur of movement that resulted in Cartega going down, she took a quick step back, her foot slipping in the snow. By sheer force of will, she managed to stay upright and slam the crowbar against the wall with all her might.

The patio door abruptly slid open. Her awkward position of leaning against the side of the house put her at a disadvantage. Yet she brought the crowbar back, aiming for Blaine's midsection, fearing she'd kill him if she struck him in the head.

Zion growled low in her throat, lunging forward and grabbing Blaine's leg with her teeth.

"What the—" His curse was cut off when the dog bit down hard. "Oww!"

Maya brought the crowbar up again, ramming the metal bar into his gut. With Zion holding on to his leg, her thrust sent him reeling. Zion eventually let go, backing away but keeping her blue gaze on Blaine. Maybe it was her imagination, but the dog looked satisfied with the role she'd played in this tussle.

Shouldering her way through the opening of the patio door, she followed Blaine. The warmth was a blessing, but there was no time to appreciate it. Somehow, she'd managed to hang onto the crowbar. Blaine let out a howl and pulled his weapon. Before he could turn the muzzle toward her, she swung the metal rod, bringing it down on his wrist. He cried out in pain, curse words tumbling from his lips.

The gun clattered to the floor. She kicked it with her boot, sending it skittering across the wooden floor.

Right toward the injured man, who stood in the hallway off to the side of the kitchen next to Emily. He stopped the gun with his foot and their eyes met. His were an icy blue color, much like Zion's.

Before she could say a word, Blaine launched himself at her. She took his weight with a muffled oomph, and they both tumbled backward. The back of her head slammed into the patio door, near the area that was already injured.

"What are you doing?" Emily cried out in horror.

Maya didn't have time to glance at her because Blaine's hands were closing around her throat. She brought her knee up into his groin, but the padded snowsuit she wore minimized the impact.

She tried to bring the crowbar up but couldn't. Blaine let out another howl, making her realize Zion had grabbed his leg again.

His fingers loosened around her throat, providing the opening she needed. Dropping the crowbar, she wrestled her hands up between his arms to break his grip.

Then Blaine was suddenly pulled away from her. Zion still had a hold of his leg, and he went down, hitting the floor with a loud thud. From where she was slumped against the patio door, she could see how Blaine's head bounced off the floor. Not that she felt much pity for him. "Release," she croaked. "Zion, release!"

Zion let Blaine go and backed away, still growling. Thankfully, Blaine didn't move, appearing to be out cold.

A flash of hot anger darkened Doug's eyes as he whirled toward the injured man standing beside Emily. He was holding on to the wall and bending over to pick up the gun, but he was a moment too late.

"Don't!" Doug barked. He had his weapon in hand and was pointing it directly at the wounded perp. "Let Emily go."

The wounded man froze, then slowly lifted his hands palms forward. Then he went a step further and kicked the gun down the hall behind him.

"Doug!" Emily rushed forward as if to throw herself into his arms, but then stopped when her brother held out his hand. His gaze appeared locked on the only perp standing, and Maya feared he might just finish him off.

"Stay back," Doug said harshly.

"Over here, Emily," she said, her throat sore from being gripped by Blaine. She pulled her gloves off and fished in her pocket for her weapon. "Stand over here."

"Who are you?" Emily asked in confusion.

Apparently, being covered from head to toe had made it difficult for Emily to recognize her. She pulled the face mask away. "Maya Sullivan, Kendra's sister." Despite the warmth of the fire, she was still shivering.

Cold air streamed through the open front and patio doors. Her fingers trembled so badly she doubted she'd be able to shoot if needed. Thankfully, she didn't think that would be necessary. "Do me a favor and close the patio door."

"Maya!" Emily looked relieved to see her. The younger woman quickly closed the patio door, then stepped over Blaine to get to the front door.

Blaine abruptly grabbed Emily's foot, stopping her.

"No!" Maya lunged forward, stomping hard on Blaine's stomach, bringing the muzzle of her gun up to his face. "Let her go!"

Blaine did so, his eyes wide. Then he smirked. "You wouldn't shoot me."

"Don't bet on that." She stepped back, still holding her weapon in a two-handed grip. At this range, she couldn't miss.

She hoped.

"Emily, we need rope to tie him up," Doug said calmly. He glanced at her, nodded with appreciation, then added, "See what you can find."

"O-okay." Emily crossed to the kitchen, this time making sure to give Blaine and the injured perp a wide berth. "But how did you get here?"

"Long story," Doug said tersely. "For now, we need to get these two men secured. Then I'll go out to get Cartega. I don't think I killed him, but the cold might do the job for me if I don't get out there soon."

"Will this work?" Emily held up a ball of twine.

"Yes." Doug eyed Blaine. "Roll onto your stomach and put your hands behind your back. Don't give me a reason to shoot."

Blaine's expression was sullen, but seeing Maya's gun, he

slowly rolled over onto his stomach. Emily bent over to secure the twine around his wrists.

"Tighten that binding," Maya said.

Emily didn't look happy but did as she was told.

"Now the wounded guy," Doug said. "Tie his wrists behind his back too."

"Oh, but he can't . . ." Emily stopped at her brother's searing look. "Okay."

Before Emily could cross over, the injured man spoke for the first time. "You may want to get out of here, before our associate arrives."

Their associate? Maya glanced at Doug, then back at the injured man. Was he making that up to scare them?

If not, their nightmare wasn't over.

14

Doug stared at the blue-eyed perp. The mystery man might be wounded, but Doug didn't believe for one second the guy was harmless. In his opinion, the perp looked more dangerous than Blaine and Cartega combined.

"Emily, tie his wrists, tightly." He ignored the perp's statement about more bad guys being on the way. The weather would give them plenty of time to prepare for a new arrival.

He hoped.

Emily didn't look happy as she took a length of twine to bind his wrists as directed. Doug didn't care for the way his sister seemed so protective of the guy. Maybe she'd be that way toward all her patients, but somehow, he doubted it. This guy had gotten to her.

Because she had a soft heart? Or was she suffering from a form of Stockholm syndrome? Either way, he lowered his weapon once the wounded man had been secured. Two down and one more to go. "Sit down," he ordered.

The injured man sat.

He turned to Maya. "Get Blaine into another chair. I need to head back out to grab Cartega."

Maya was already pulling her ex-husband to his feet. She pushed him toward the chair he'd been sitting in earlier. Zion was looking at Maya expectantly, so when Blaine was taken care of, she crossed to the dog. "Good girl," she said in a low voice. Then she pulled the bunny from her pocket and tossed it into the air. Zion leaped up to grab it, shaking her head from side to side as if daring Maya to yank it back. Then the dog trotted around the room with her prize. It would have been funny if not for the seriousness of the situation.

"Is that how you found us? Did Zion track me here?" Emily asked.

"Zion helped, but Maya was the one who put it together." He crossed to the front door and pulled it open. The blast of cold wind brutally slammed against his face. He still wasn't warm and was beginning to doubt he ever would be.

Cartega was lying on the ground where he'd left him. A thin layer of snow covered his body, indicating the drug dealer hadn't moved.

Earlier, when he'd pounded on the wall to draw the guy outside, Doug had lunged forward, bringing the hammer down hard on Cartega's extended arm. He'd heard the crack as the guy's wrist snapped in two. Cartega had screamed and dropped the gun, grabbing at his injured arm. Ignoring the flash of guilt, Doug had taken advantage of his pain long enough to strike him on the back of the head. His goal was to disable him long enough that he could get inside to help Maya.

He hadn't intended to kill him. Yet the way Cartega was lying face down on the ground covered with snow wasn't a good sign. He reached down, grabbed the guy by the back of his shirt, and lifted him up.

Cartega's body was limp. He didn't move or seem to know Doug was there. After rolling him over onto his back, Doug reached down to check his pulse.

And found nothing.

The drug dealer was dead. He swallowed hard, hoping God would forgive him. With a heavy sigh, he stood and turned to head back inside. Reviewing the steps he'd taken wasn't helpful. This wasn't the time to dwell on things he could have done differently. Cartega had chosen his life of crime. Even after being put in prison, the first thing he'd done upon his release was to return to his old ways. Only this time, Cartega's drug dealing had morphed into kidnapping and murder.

The only good news was that with Cartega out of the equation, he had more confidence in their ability to hold off the so-called associate who allegedly was on his way to the cabin through the blizzard.

If the wounded perp was telling the truth. He didn't trust the injured guy as far as he could throw him.

He stepped inside the cabin, closing and locking the front door behind him. All four of the occupants turned to look at him expectantly. Pushing away from the door, he shrugged. "Cartega didn't make it."

Emily's eyes rounded in horror, and she darted a worried glance toward the injured perp. A bloody stain leeched through his long-sleeved woolen T-shirt, but the guy seemed oblivious to any discomfort.

Maya didn't seem surprised by the news. She had shrugged out of her coat and was kneeling with a towel beside Zion. The booties had been removed, and the husky didn't seem to mind as Maya used the terrycloth to warm the dog's paws. Zion simply held one paw up at a time as if this was a familiar routine.

And it probably was. He stepped farther into the room and took off his coat too. The layer of snow that covered his winter gear made puddles on the floor, so he tossed his coat in the far corner, well out of the way. His feet were still numb, but he didn't remove his boots yet. Instead, he turned his attention back to the stranger. "What's your name?"

For a moment, the perp's blue eyes flashed with anger, then it was gone. He lifted his good shoulder in a nonchalant shrug. "Owen."

Doug waited for a last name, but it didn't come.

"Owen was shot," Emily said, breaking the silence. "I removed the slug from his shoulder, but he's fighting infection. We really need to get him to the hospital as soon as possible."

"No hospital," Owen growled. "I'll survive."

Emily rolled her eyes. But before she could argue, Doug interrupted. "Save it. We're not going anywhere. The storm is getting worse, and the SUV is well over a mile away. He'll never make it that far, and I'm not carrying him." He held Owen's blue gaze. "Nobody will be arriving anytime soon."

Owen looked away as if he didn't care one way or the other. And maybe his wound was infected as the guy looked pale with beads of sweat popping out on his forehead.

"I really should get Owen back to bed," Emily said with a frown. "He's not looking so good."

"No, stay back," he barked when she moved as if to untie the guy. "Don't touch him. He can sit there for a while yet." He knew he sounded crabby. Because he was. He was also cold, hungry, and exhausted.

And the day was barely half over.

"But Doug . . ." she protested.

He clenched his jaw to keep from snapping at her. "We've been outside for hours, Em. On the road first, then hiking through the storm. Do you think you could make coffee and throw something together for us to eat?"

His sister's expression softened. "Yes, of course." She glanced at Owen, but then moved past him to reach the coffee maker. "Coming right up."

Blaine hadn't spoken a single word since learning of Cartega's death, which Doug took as a blessing. He could tell the guy was a whiner, much like Craig Olsen had been. Both were far from being competent criminals.

Moving to the wood stove, he bent and grabbed a log. He opened the door, shielding his face from the blast of heat, and tossed it inside. After closing the stove tightly, he sat on the coffee table and unlaced his boots. His fingers were tingling with warmth, but he still couldn't feel his toes. Glancing at Maya, he was glad to see she'd removed her boots, too, and had her feet facing the fire.

Seconds later, he was warming his toes too.

For a moment, his gaze locked with hers. He wanted to kiss her in the worst way but settled for a crooked smile. "We made it."

"Yeah, we did." She smiled back. He wanted to believe the awareness simmering between them wasn't one sided. They'd struggled and survived against the odds. She and Zion had been amazing, the best partners he could have asked for.

In that moment, he knew he'd never forget her.

Yet he couldn't focus on his feelings now. There was still work to do. As his toes began to come back to life, he glanced at Blaine. The guy's expression was grim as he darted dark glances toward Maya as if upset at how easily she'd taken him down. As he should be. Although Maya had help from her protective K9.

The way Zion's blue eyes remained focused on Blaine made him smile. The dog knew Blaine was the bad guy, and Doug suspected if the guy made a move toward Maya, the husky would jump him.

Blaine seemed to sense that too.

"Here you go," Emily said, bringing two steaming mugs of coffee into the living room. She handed one to Maya, then turned to him. "There are several cans of beef stew available if you're interested."

"Very interested," he said, taking the coffee. He wrapped his fingers around the mug nearly moaning with pleasure. He would never take being warm and having shelter for granted ever again. "Thanks."

Emily rested her hand on his shoulder for a moment. "Thank you for coming to find me. I never imagined you'd hike through the snowstorm."

He patted her hand. "You should thank Maya. I wouldn't have made it without her help."

"We worked together; no thanks needed." Maya sipped her coffee. As Emily turned to head back to the kitchen, she said, "Maybe we should interrogate these guys to figure out what is really going on."

Blaine scowled at her comment. "Nothing is going on. Your dog bit me, and you killed Cartega for no reason. We didn't hurt the girl. We just needed her to care for Owen."

"You may not have hurt Emily, but you killed Stevie," Maya said. "We found his body."

Blaine flushed red, then shrugged. "I don't know what you're talking about."

"Yeah, you killed him," Doug said firmly. "And you used his own gun to do the deed. But I'm not worried. It's only a matter of time until you go down for the murder. I'm sure the crime scene techs have recovered your DNA from the truck."

"I was never inside—" Blaine abruptly stopped, catching himself. Then he lamely repeated, "I don't know anything about that."

"And you assaulted me," Maya said. "Either doing the deed yourself or getting Stevie to do it."

Blaine stared at the floor.

"Fool," Owen said harshly. "No wonder they were hot on our trail."

Doug turned to glance at the injured man. Owen had claimed their associate was on the way, indicating the guy was their boss. Yet his gut was telling him that Owen was the real man in charge.

"Yeah, it's really tough to get good help these days, isn't it?" he said, watching Owen closely. "Especially out here in the middle of nowhere. Looks to me like you ended up with amateur hour."

Owen's blue eyes didn't give anything away, but Doug could sense his frustration. Likely he'd been the one to demand they kidnap Emily to care for him. As the wounded perp remained silent, Doug got the impression he was planning his next move.

Oh yeah, there wasn't a doubt in his mind that Owen was the guy in charge. The perp had to be lying about anyone else being on the way. It wasn't likely anyone was willing to brave the elements to get to the cabin.

But Doug would remain alert just in case.

They'd made it this far. And despite feeling bad over Cartega's death, Doug silently promised he wouldn't hesitate to shoot to kill if additional bad guys managed to get through the storm to arrive on their doorstep.

Better to eliminate the threat before anyone else was hurt.

THE WARMTH of the cabin had finally reached Maya's core. But with the heat came a weariness that was hard to fight back. She'd used up every bit of her energy to keep moving forward and wanted nothing more than to curl up for a long nap.

She could see the weariness on Doug's features too.

"Hey, nurse. Fix my leg," Blaine said in a petulant tone. "That stupid dog bit me."

"Shut up." Doug's voice was harsh. "Or I'll find something to use as a gag to keep you quiet."

Maya arched a brow at the alarm in Emily's gaze as she stood warming the beef stew on the stove. Doug's sister was too soft-hearted for her own good.

"I'll take a look," Maya offered, although touching Blaine was the last thing she wanted to do.

Blaine opened his mouth, glanced at Doug's threatening glare, then closed it again. He moved in the chair so that his injured leg was before her.

Setting her empty coffee mug aside, Maya bent over to examine Zion's bite marks. Thankfully, they weren't as bad as she'd feared. Zion's teeth had dug deep mostly because of the way Blaine had tried to fight her off.

The wounds were red, though, and she knew they could easily become worse. Dog bites were notorious for causing infections.

"I'd better clean this," she said with a sigh.

Doug frowned but didn't protest as she made her way to the kitchen. Her socks grew damp from the melted snow puddles on the floor. Once she'd taken care of Blaine's wounds, she'd search for replacements for herself and Doug. She abhorred the idea of heading back out into the storm, but they needed to be ready just in case.

The beef stew smelled wonderful. She filled a bowl with hot water, found soap and a washcloth, then returned to the living room. Blaine's expression was sullen as she quickly cleaned the bites. Her ex-husband was obviously biting his tongue, clearly believing Doug's threat to gag him.

Emily washed her hands, filled two bowls with steaming beef stew and carried them into the living room. Maya sat in the chair Cartega had used, gratefully accepting the food.

Doug cradled his bowl on his lap too. He met her gaze, and she knew he was silently asking her to pray.

"Dear Lord Jesus, we thank You for keeping us all safe in Your care. Thank You for guiding us through the storm and please continue to watch over us as we make our way home. Amen."

"Amen," Doug echoed.

Blaine snorted with derision, but Maya ignored him. She took a bite of the steaming meat, burning her tongue. The hearty mix of beef, potatoes, and carrots were perfect to replace the calories they'd burned getting there.

Especially since she feared there was more to come.

She and Doug ate in silence for several minutes. When she was finished, she set her bowl aside and rose to her feet. She took a few minutes to spread her coat out near the fire. Then crossed the room to grab Doug's discarded coat. Both items needed to be warmed and dried out if they were going to survive another encounter with the storm.

She set both their boots near the fire too. When that was done, she turned and headed into the main bedroom. She'd figured the one Owen had been using was the primary room and began rummaging through the drawers.

There were plenty of items to choose from.

She removed her snow pants and quickly drew on an oversized pair of men's sweats over her jeans. Then she pulled off her wet socks in favor of warm woolen ones. She looked for slippers of some sort but didn't see any.

Poking her head in the bathroom, she found plenty of towels. To keep her feet dry, she hauled them along with her soggy snow pants into the main living area. She used the towels to mop up the pools of water, then put the snow pants along the back of the wood-burning stove. She shrugged when she saw Doug watching her.

"We need to stay warm and dry. There are more clothes in the dresser and closet back there." She jerked her thumb to the main bedroom behind the kitchen. "You should change into whatever fits."

He grunted, finished his beef stew, then rose. "Okay. You're the expert."

If they'd been alone, she'd have teased him, but Emily's curious gaze had her holding her tongue. She picked up the dirty dishes and carried them to the sink.

Drawing Emily aside, she lowered her voice to ask, "Are you okay? Did they hurt you?"

Emily shot a telling glance toward Owen. "I'm fine. I was scared at first, but they truly only wanted me to care for Owen's injury."

Maya nodded, holding the younger woman's gaze. "I'm here if you need to talk. None of this is your fault."

"I know. It's just . . ." Again, she glanced at Owen. He sat with his head down, his eyes closed as if willing himself to stay upright. "I was panicked and fought when they dragged me into the truck. They tied me up until we got to the motel.

That's where they had Owen. They released me to care for him. And I have."

"You did a good job of keeping calm," Maya said. "I'm proud of you."

"Thanks, but that's my training." Emily brushed off the praise. "Look at him, Maya. I hate seeing him suffer. You need to convince Doug to let me take him back to the bedroom. His wound is bleeding again. I'd like to change the bandages."

Maya sighed. "He's a dangerous man, Emily. Just because he's wounded doesn't mean he can't hurt you."

"He won't." She sounded completely convinced. "Besides, he's too weak to do much damage, even if he wanted to."

Maya highly doubted that was true. Sure, Owen's pale skin and sweat-beaded brow were difficult to fake, but she sensed an inner strength that would easily carry him forward under the right set of circumstances.

"I'll try." She turned to refill her coffee mug. Keeping busy was one way to stay awake. Downing more coffee was another.

It wasn't easy to stay focused on the potential danger now that she was warm, dry, and had food in her belly. She stepped aside as Emily turned her attention to Owen.

"Would you like more ibuprofen?" she asked. "You're about due for another dose."

"Yeah. Thanks." Owen's gruff voice had softened. Maya frowned, wondering if his gratitude was real.

Or an act to sway Emily into taking his side.

She washed the dishes as Emily hovered over Owen, giving him the ibuprofen tablets and water. She took the glass and washed that, too, wishing she could convince Emily to keep her distance.

Some perps excelled at manipulating people, and she feared Owen was using Emily's caring nature against her.

"I feel much better," Doug said as he strode into the kitchen. He wore a lambskin-lined plaid shirt over his long johns and had borrowed a pair of the woolen socks. He gestured to his feet. "I don't think I have any frostbite, but if we'd had been out there much longer, I'm sure I would have lost a few toes."

Emily looked alarmed. "Frostbite can be serious."

"No lie," he agreed. "Maya, are you okay?"

"Yes." She'd checked her fingers and toes thoroughly as well. "We have God to thank for protecting us."

Emily darted a curious look from Maya to Doug. Then she nodded in agreement. "Amen to that."

Owen groaned and slumped to the side. Maya shot him a suspicious glance, but Emily rushed over.

"Owen? He's burning up with fever!" Emily swung toward her brother. "Doug, you need to let me get him into bed. Tie his arm to the bedpost if you must, but we can't just let him suffer like this."

Doug glanced at her for guidance. She shrugged. "Pretty hard to fake a fever. I don't see how it matters if he's here or in the bedroom tied to the bedpost."

"Fine." Doug scowled as he reached over to untie Owen's wrists. "Don't try anything or I'll put you down so fast your head will spin."

Owen barely grunted in response, swaying in the chair. Maya was tempted to pull her weapon just in case, but Owen didn't put up a fight. He couldn't stand under his own power, so Doug slung one of his arms over his shoulder to steady him.

Emily took the other side. Between the two half siblings,

they were able to half carry/half drag the wounded man down the hall to the bedroom.

"You should untie me too," Blaine complained. "My wrists are killing me."

"Not a chance." She returned to the living room where Zion was stretched out on the floor near the stove. Her K9 opened one blue eye, then closed it again.

Her dog was exhausted too. They all needed to rest and recover.

Yet even knowing that, she found herself moving through the cabin, going from one window to the next. The swirling snow hadn't lessened one iota. Just the opposite. The gusts of wind caused a total whiteout.

She shivered, grateful they were warm and safe inside.

"Come on," Blaine cajoled. "What if I lose my arms? How am I gonna work then?"

She whirled to glare at him. "You don't work now from what I can tell. You're here for the easy money, aren't you? First, you convinced Stevie to stalk me, then when you realized I was helping Doug find his sister, you decided to attack me. You're scum. Worse than scum."

His face flushed red. "I don't know what you're talking about."

She turned away, knowing there was no point in even trying. He was a liar, a cheat, and a crook.

Thank goodness she'd gotten divorced when she had.

She made another sweep of the room, going from the front of the cabin to the back patio doors. As she turned away, she thought she saw a glimpse of light.

Probably a reflection off the glass. Still, she lifted her hands to cup them around her face to peer outside.

And saw it again. A bouncing light. It took a moment for the image to register.

A snow machine!

"Doug!" She whirled and quickly shoved her feet into her boots. Then she drew her gun. "Hurry! Someone's approaching the cabin on a snowmobile!"

"Where?" Doug ran into the room, his gaze full of alarm.

"Coming in from the back." She gestured to the patio doors. "I hate to say it, but I think that's the associate Owen mentioned."

Doug grimaced and reached for his boots. "Stay here. I need you and Zion to protect Emily."

"I don't think you should go alone," she protested. "He could have a rider behind him. Or another sled may be on the way too."

Doug's expression was grim as he grabbed his coat. "Keep Emily safe," he repeated, then quickly turned and headed out the front door, disappearing into the swirling snow.

15

The wind smacked him in the face as he hurried toward the garage. It seemed as if the snowfall was lessening, but the wind was still fierce. He didn't know if the snow machine had gas in the tank, or if it even worked, but he needed to try.

There was no point in trying to be quiet, so he hauled the garage door upward and headed inside. He'd remembered the snow machine had the key in the ignition. He straddled the seat and took precious seconds to figure out the controls. He had gone snowmobiling a few times in the past, but not recently. And not with a sled of this make and model.

He found the ignition switch. The engine fired up. He sent up a prayer of thanks as he glanced around for a helmet. With the wind and snow, he'd need the face shield to see where he was going. Spying a bag on the floor, he bent over and opened it. There was a helmet inside, along with additional gear. He wouldn't have minded donning more protection, but there was no time. Grabbing the helmet, he pulled it over his head and secured the strap under his chin.

Driving the snow machine out of the garage made a large scraping sound as the skis dragged across the cement floor. But once he hit the snow-covered ground outside, the belt underneath his seat found traction, and he flew forward.

Faster than snowshoes, he thought as he cranked on the handlebar. The front skis turned nicely over the snow, enabling him to head around the back of the property. Not as quiet as snowshoes, but he could cover the distance much quicker.

Of course, that meant the guy on the other sled could do the same.

The bobbing headlight of the snow machine coming toward him was gaining ground. Doug used his thumb to hit the gas, speeding forward to narrow the distance between them. He only had a vague plan. There was no phone service, so the associate wouldn't know who he was until they were up close. Even then, with their respective helmets in place, identifying faces would be nearly impossible.

He'd pretend to be Blaine, letting the new guy know Owen's condition had taken a turn for the worse. Then he'd take him down.

As plans went, it wasn't stellar. But it was the best he could come up with.

As the sleds grew closer, Doug lifted his hand in greeting, the way he'd assumed Blaine would. They must know each other, right? Then he executed a wide turn—sharp turns were impossible with snow machines—so that he could come up alongside the other sled.

The driver slowed his speed, glancing over at him. "What's going on?" he shouted over the roar of their two engines.

"Owen's dying!" he shouted back. "The nurse is freaking out!"

The stranger slowed his speed a bit, so Doug did the same. He kept a few feet between their sleds so he would have room to maneuver. "Who cares? Taking her had been stupid anyway. We need to get out of here as soon as the storm clears!"

Fighting among the ranks? If so, he may have misjudged Owen's position within the organization. The glow from the wood-burning stove was a beacon in the storm. They were getting closer to the cabin now, and he could easily make out the silhouette of Blaine seated in the chair.

Would the stranger recognize Blaine's blond hair? He swallowed hard, knowing he was running out of time. To prevent this guy from getting inside and possibly hurting Emily or Maya, he needed to make his move. Pressing his thumb on the gas button, he abruptly sent the sled surging forward. Then he wrenched the front skis to the side, cutting the second sled off.

The stranger had little choice but to try to make a counter move to go behind him. He wrenched the handlebars a few seconds too late. The stranger's front skis didn't clear the rear of his sled. The impact sent Doug reeling. He clung to the handlebars with all his strength and fought to keep his seat.

Thankfully, the stranger wasn't as prepared. He flew off his sled, landing in the deep snow. Doug released the throttle and quickly yanked his gloves off with his teeth. Pulling his weapon from his pocket, he shouted, "DEA! Don't move!"

The stranger didn't listen. He fumbled in his pocket, likely for a weapon.

"Don't force me to shoot!" Even as he shouted the words,

the stranger pulled his gun free, turning the muzzle toward him. Doug fired twice, aiming for center mass. The impact of the slugs sent the perp reeling backward.

Doug fought his way through the deep snow to reach the stranger's side. He didn't see the gun, but to his surprise, the man on the ground let out a low groan. Ignoring the freezing cold on his bare hands, he lifted the guy's face shield.

And stared in shock when he recognized Sergeant Tom Howell of the Cody police department.

"Are you wearing a vest?" He reached down to pull the man upright. The fact that Howell was still breathing indicated he must have body armor underneath the snowsuit. "Do you have other weapons on you?"

"You shot me!" Howell accused.

"You pulled a gun on a fed!" Doug stared down at him. "I can't believe you're a part of this!"

There was a moment's pause, before Howell said, "I'm not. I'm working undercover. I thought you were that hothead Blaine, so I played along." Howell put a hand to his chest. "Man, it hurts to take two slugs to the vest."

Doug narrowed his gaze, unsure if he should believe him. He bent and continued patting him down. Finding no other weapons, he took a step back. "Get up. We're going to hash this out inside."

"Don't blow my cover," Howell said, struggling to his feet. He glanced around as if searching for his gun, but it was nowhere nearby.

"Don't bother. I won't let you keep the weapon anyway." Still unsure if Howell was telling the truth, he gestured to the sled. "Get back on. I'll follow you in. Don't try anything or I'll take you down."

"Hey, no need for threats. I'm on your side," Howell said

in a voice that lacked conviction. He was clearly hurting from taking the rounds but managed to climb back onto the snow machine.

Doug straddled his and grasped the handles. They had built-in hand warmers, which was nice as his fingers felt like frozen fish sticks. Yet he needed to be able to shoot, so he didn't bother putting his gloves back on.

The machines weren't badly damaged, the snow had blunted most of the impact, yet he could see one of Howell's ski tips was broken off. Even so, Howell's snow machine moved forward without difficulty. They weren't far from the cabin and managed to get there in a few minutes.

He pulled his weapon and aimed it at Howell when the cop turned to face him. Howell continued to act as if they were buddies. "Smart to keep your weapon trained on me. I can't afford for you to blow my cover."

"Yeah, so you said." He gestured with the tip of his gun. "Move."

Howell hesitated, then trudged up to the patio doors. Doug could see Maya hovering on the other side. He removed his helmet and scowled, hoping she'd stay back.

She didn't. She opened the door and gaped when she recognized Howell. "Tom! What are you doing here?"

"Move aside," Doug said. "Find that twine so we can tie him up too."

Howell stepped into the cabin, lifting his helmet off his head. "You idiot," he said to Blaine. "This is your fault."

Zion began to growl low in her throat. Doug was surprised, as he didn't remember the dog growling at Howell before. The K9's gaze was locked on Howell. Zion let out three sharp barks, then resumed her growling. It took a moment to realize why she was reacting to Howell.

Had the cop been the one to hit Maya over the head?

The way Howell backed away, shooting a quick glance at Maya, confirmed his suspicions. No way was Howell working undercover.

The local cop was just as involved, if not more so than Blaine, Cartega, and Owen.

As if reading his thoughts, Howell launched himself at Doug, slamming into him before he could get a shot off. From the corner of his eye, he watched as Zion attacked Howell, biting down on his leg. The cop let out a scream. Then Maya was there, her weapon pressed into his temple.

"Let him go or I'll shoot," she said calmly. "Zion, hold him."

The dog did not release her grip. Howell sat back, shifting his weight off Doug, and lifted his hands in surrender. Doug wiggled out from underneath him, retrieving his weapon from the floor. Annoyed with being caught off guard, he gave Maya a nod of thanks.

"Keep your hands where I can see them," Maya said. "You're outnumbered and outgunned. We won't hesitate to shoot."

"I shot him twice when he pulled a gun on me outside, but he's wearing a vest." Doug glanced over to see Emily hovering in the kitchen, her eyes wide as she watched the activity. "I need more twine."

"I figured. Here." Emily tossed the roll toward him.

"Have you seen this man before?" He glanced at his half sister as he bound Howell's wrists. "Has he been involved?"

"I saw him at Wild Bill's," Emily said. "But not since then."

When he'd finished tying Howell, he lifted the guy up and set him down hard on the chair next to Blaine. Then he asked, "I have three of you in custody now. Cartega is dead. I want to know how many others are involved in whatever you have going on here."

Blaine and Howell glanced at each other but said nothing.

Doug sighed. He hadn't really expected them to talk. Being a cop, Howell knew they had the right to remain silent. He didn't want to believe other Cody police officers were involved, but having Howell arriving on scene changed things.

The immediate danger was over. But once they had cell service, he'd need to get in touch with the federal agents in Cheyenne. He was operating way outside his jurisdiction, although he'd do it again in a heartbeat. He'd found Emily, and that was all that mattered.

But from here on out, the case would need to be handled by the local authorities. He wasn't sure what they were up to prior to Owen being shot and kidnapping Emily. At the moment, he didn't even care.

For the first time in his career, he couldn't wait to hand these guys off to become someone else's problem.

He was done with them.

MAYA GLARED at Howell in disgust. He was a disgrace to the uniform, and a traitor to every law enforcement officer out there. "You assaulted me outside my SUV."

Tom Howell looked away without saying anything. But the angry glance he shot toward Zion confirmed her suspicions. She'd assumed Blaine had hired Stevie to take her out. And she suspected Stevie had been the one following her around town. But Tom was the one who'd attempted to eliminate her from the equation.

A stunt that had almost worked.

Doug removed his coat and boots, setting them near the wood-burning stove. Then he gestured for her to follow him down to the other two bedrooms located on the other side of the cabin.

"Howell tried to tell me he was working undercover," he said. "That's a lie; he pulled a gun on me after I told him I was with the DEA."

"I agree, although other than Zion's nose recognizing his scent, we don't have any proof." She lowered her hand to pet the husky's springy fur. "I'm glad you're okay. Going after him like that was a risky move."

"I wanted him under control before allowing him inside the cabin." He smiled ruefully. "And that pretty much worked until he caught me off guard. You're a great partner, Maya. I was glad you had my back in there."

"Anytime." She held his gaze wishing there was something she could say that would convince him to stay. "I care about you, Doug."

"I care about you too." He reached for her hand. "I wouldn't have found Emily without you and Zion."

She didn't want his gratitude over her SAR work but forced a nod. Clearly, he was keeping their relationship professional. "I'm glad we found her. We had a chance to talk earlier in the kitchen, and she claims they didn't hurt her."

"That's good." He scowled. "I don't like the way she hovers over Owen, though."

"Yeah, I noticed," she admitted. "I'm sure he's been nice to her, and maybe he even kept the others from hurting her."

That possibility seemed to relieve his fears. "I still feel a little guilty over Cartega."

"Don't." She clung to his hand, admiring his sense of honor and justice. She understood where he was coming from. No cop appreciated being forced to kill a perp. Yet their training also meant they wouldn't hesitate to do just that if needed. "It wasn't your fault. If we weren't in the middle of a blizzard, he may have survived."

"Yeah. Maybe. I just hope God can forgive me." He stared down at her.

"He will, Doug. Jesus died to forgive our sins." She reached up to kiss his cheek.

But he turned and quickly captured her mouth with his. Her heart soared with hope. So much for being professional. She wrapped her arms around his neck and drew him closer, reveling in their kiss.

"Doug!" Emily shouted in alarm. "Hurry, he's getting away!"

Doug broke off from their embrace with a low groan. She understood his annoyance.

"Who?" she asked. They had secured Howell and Blaine, hadn't they? Doug shook his head and headed back out to the living area. She followed close on his heels.

Outside, a man dressed from head to toe in protective gear straddled one of the snow machines. Then in the blink of an eye, he was speeding away from the cabin.

Not Blaine or Tom as they sat silently in their respective chairs. Owen. Somehow, he'd managed to find the clothing he needed, even grabbing Howell's helmet.

"Hurry, you have to catch up to him," Emily pleaded, her eyes wide. "He's sick. He's not going to make it. He'll die out there!"

Doug sighed. "I'm not going after him, Em. He made his choice."

Emily's green eyes, so much like Doug's, filled with tears. Then she turned away, burying her face in her hands.

Maya glanced at Doug. They were both thinking the same thing. Maybe it was better this way. Emily had gotten far too attached to Owen.

"I'll take the sled to the SUV," she offered as Doug watched helplessly as Emily cried. "Zion can ride in front. She's done it before. You should stay here."

"No, I'll go." He sighed. "She needs time to get over this."

Maya agreed, then frowned as she glanced out the front picture window. Three snow machines were coming down the driveway toward the cabin.

More bad guys? She quickly pulled her gun. Doug did too.

"You take the front door." Doug's expression was grim. "I'll head out around back to cover the side."

The lead sled slid around the curve, giving her a glimpse of the logo along the side. She grabbed Doug's arm. "Wait. They're my siblings from the ranch."

"Are you sure?" Doug followed her gaze. The sleds were closer now, and the snow had diminished to the point that they could see the Sullivan K9 logo clearly. Doug looked shocked. "Our phones haven't worked since the storm hit. How did they find us?"

"They probably tracked me by using the GPS in the SUV." She grinned and slid her weapon into the waistband of her oversized borrowed sweatpants. "The calvary has arrived."

Of course, Chase was in the lead with her brothers Shane and Trevor riding shotgun. She opened the door to let them in.

"You've been AWOL," Chase accused. Then he noticed

the others in the room, including the two men sitting with their arms tied behind their backs. "What's going on?"

"It's a long story," Maya said. Zion bounded forward to greet her brothers, wagging her tail in joy. She'd noticed they hadn't brought their K9's along, likely due to the weather. "I'm glad to see you guys. Oh, this is Doug Bridges, he's with the DEA." She noticed Emily had managed to stop crying. The young woman swiped at her face, then offered a wan smile. Emily had been out to the ranch to visit Kendra, so she knew her brothers. "Doug, this is Chase, Shane, and Trevor."

"Nice to meet you," Doug said. "Your sister and Zion were amazing in helping me find Emily. We have these guys in custody." He jerked his thumb at Tom and Blaine. "Unfortunately, one man is dead, and the other escaped a few minutes ago on a snowmobile."

"You could go after him," Emily said again. "I mean, if you wanted to get him into custody."

Maya inwardly winced. "Not happening. I'm sure he'll eventually end up at the hospital."

Emily wrapped her arms around herself and nodded as if finally accepting the truth. Owen was gone, and the odds he'd survive were slim.

It took a while to come to a consensus on their next steps. There were three sleds and eight people plus a dog needing transport from the cabin. All while keeping their two perps restrained.

Chase finally held up his hand. "Okay, here's how this is going to work. We'll need to take several trips. We'll put the two bad guys on one sled. We'll secure the driver's hands to the handlebars, then tie them together. Doug, you're armed as I am, so we'll escort them to the SUV. Then we'll come back for Maya, Zion, and Emily. The last trip will be to grab Trevor and Shane."

"Why are we last?" Trevor complained.

"Yeah, we're the good guys," Shane added.

Chase rolled his eyes. "Stuff it. Take time to secure the place while we're doing the transports."

"Yeah, yeah," Shane grumbled.

Maya crossed over to Emily once Chase and Doug had taken the two prisoners outside. "Are you okay?"

"Fine." Fresh tears welled in her eyes. "I'm being stupid about this."

Maya shrugged. "As your brother once told me, emotions are rarely logical. Besides, I'm sure Owen will find a way to get the help he needs."

"If he lives that long." Emily sighed. "I don't know why I'm upset. As Doug said, he made his choice."

Maya gave Emily a tight hug. "You're safe. That's all that matters."

The various trips back and forth to the SUVs didn't take long. The drive back to Cody was another story. The highway was treacherous. The snowfall had dwindled, but the wind still howled. Twice they almost got bogged down in snowdrifts. Chase had the added difficulty of pulling a trailer of snow machines. As they approached the city, though, their cell service was restored.

Maya listened as Doug spoke to the FBI office in Cheyenne about the two men, one a local cop, that he had in custody. He went on to mention the body of Cartega that still needed to be recovered, along with the man named Owen who'd escaped.

By the time they'd dropped Blaine and Tom off at the local jail, much to the dismay of the officers who'd worked alongside their sergeant, and returned to the hotel, darkness had fallen in earnest.

"Head home," she told Chase as he sat in the driver's seat of his SUV. "I'll be right behind you."

Her brother scowled. "We'll wait."

"Suit yourself." Maya wondered if she was being as foolish as Emily as she and Zion followed Doug and Emily into the Great Frontier Hotel. The suite was still under her name, so Doug quickly handed his card over instead. After explaining to Emily about the gunfire that had damaged her front door, Doug had convinced Emily to stay at the hotel until they could get the door repaired.

"I need a few minutes," Emily said, the moment they'd gotten inside. She headed straight for the closest bedroom, closing the door firmly behind her.

"I hope she gets over that guy," Doug muttered.

"She will." Maya stood with Zion, trying to find the strength to say goodbye. "Chase is waiting, so I need to hit the road. He's worried the trip to the ranch will be just as perilous as the ride back."

Doug's expression turned serious. "Maybe everyone should bunk down in the hotel for the night."

She shook her head. "Chase will want to get back. They didn't bring their dogs, and we have horses to care for as well." She forced a smile. "You and Emily will be fine from here on. I'm glad I was able to help. Take care of yourself, Doug."

"Maya, wait," he protested as she turned away. "I—when will I see you again?"

She arched a brow. "You don't live here. I'm sure once you get Emily's house repaired, you'll head back to Milwaukee."

"What if I don't? Head back to Milwaukee, I mean." He

closed the distance between them, reaching for her hands. "You might think I'm crazy, but I've fallen in love with you."

She felt her jaw drop and quickly tried to cover her reaction. "We barely know each other."

"True, we only know that we're both strong willed, determined, good cops and dedicated to our families." He tightened his grip on her hands. "I think I know more about you than I did my ex-wife. She didn't have a quarter of your integrity, Maya. I'm thirty-seven and have just realized how much I don't want to spend the rest of my life alone."

"Doug..." She sighed. As much as she wanted to believe him, she didn't want him to give up his life for her. "What are you going to do out here? Take a job as a Cody cop?" She smiled teasingly. "I hear they have a job opening."

"I'll apply first thing tomorrow," he said, his gaze somber. "Please give me a chance, Maya. Give us a chance."

Surprised, she searched his gaze. "You're serious about relocating here?"

"Yes. And not just because Emily needs me." He glanced toward the closed bedroom door. "She'll be fine. It's you, Maya. I want to spend time with you."

She couldn't help nodding in agreement. "I want that, too, Doug. But I hate the thought of you starting over as a Cody cop. There must be another way..."

"Doesn't matter." He glanced at Zion, then drew her into his arms. Then he was kissing her again, the way he had before they'd been interrupted by Owen's escape.

After a few minutes, she forced herself to draw back. "I really need to go. Chase is waiting. But maybe you and Emily can come out to visit us at the ranch?"

"Tomorrow?" he asked, his expression hopeful. "I would love to meet the rest of your family."

"Be careful what you wish for," she joked. Then kissed

him again. "Tomorrow. You can come for the day and have dinner with us. It will be good for Emily to hang out with Kendra too."

"Done." He hugged her close. "I love you."

"Oh, Doug." What was she thinking jumping into a relationship with a man she barely knew? Yet they weren't kids. She drew back to look up at him. "I'm thirty-six, and I don't want to spend the rest of my life alone either. I'm glad God brought us together."

"Me too." He kissed her again. Zion tried to wiggle between them, as if saying it was time to go.

"I'll be in touch tomorrow," Doug said as he walked her to the main lobby doors. Zion trotted beside them. "I hope you won't change your mind."

"I won't." She could see Chase sitting in the driver's side of his SUV, waving at her impatiently. Ignoring him, she kissed Doug. "I can't wait to see you again."

Leaving him wasn't easy, but as she headed back to the ranch, she couldn't help but smile.

God had brought them together. She didn't care if things were moving fast.

She was in love.

EPILOGUE

Three weeks later...
Doug had traversed the highway between Cody and the Sullivan K9 ranch so many times over the past few weeks he figured he could make the trip with his eyes closed. Not smart in winter, though, as the wind often blew snowdrifts over the road.

Much to the dismay of Brady Finnegan and Marc Callahan, he'd resigned from his position and had accepted a job with the State of Wyoming Criminal Investigative Division, known as CID. He'd taken a pay cut, but he had plenty of money stashed away, so he wasn't too concerned. He had a nice retirement fund and would be getting some federal benefits as well.

As an added bonus, the cost of living was much lower in Wyoming. He'd sold his house in Wisconsin in record time and had that money set aside for a house that would cost only about half as much here.

The charges against Blaine and Tom Howell included kidnapping and murder. The investigation had been taken over by a Wyoming CID investigator by the name of Chuck

Kuhn. As a witness and a victim, Doug wasn't allowed to lead the investigation, but he had been helping Chuck behind the scenes. Drugs were his area of expertise, and a search warrant for both Blaine's residence and Tom's had uncovered stashes of fentanyl. Following the Cartega lead, they'd uncovered a drug ring that extended across the state between Cheyenne and Cody.

Further investigation revealed that Cartega hadn't known Emily was Doug's sister when he'd kidnapped her. There were only a handful of nursing staff in the emergency department, and grabbing Emily had been a coincidence. In hindsight, Doug had decided that Emily's being in the wrong place was part of God's plan. If he hadn't searched for Emily with Maya and Zion's help, they wouldn't have broken up the drug cartel's new business venture.

Putting Blaine and Tom in jail where they belonged.

The only missing piece of the puzzle was Owen. He'd never shown up at the local hospital in Cody or in Greybull. Doug figured he was likely dead and that they'd eventually find his body come spring. Emily seemed to have gotten over the guy and had gone out on a date with Jared Collins, one of the physician assistants at the hospital. He was hopeful she had put the kidnapping incident behind her.

As he pulled into the long driveway leading to the main ranch house, he smiled, remembering Maya's shocked expression when he'd delivered eighty-one bags of her preferred brand of dog food delivered by truck to the ranch. Her siblings had thought it was hilarious, but she'd kept saying it was too much.

Bypassing the main ranch house, which was impressive, he headed to Maya's smaller log cabin home, which happened to be the first one to the right. The ranch property had once been used as an exclusive dude ranch, so each of the siblings had their own three-bedroom cabin. There were ten cabins total, but they used one as a guest house. The main ranch house was where everyone gathered for meals cooked by the wonderful Anna.

Maya opened the door with a smile when he pulled in. Zion bounded out, eager to greet him too. He bent and ran his hands over the husky's soft fur, then continued up to the cabin.

"Doug, it's good to see you."

"Likewise." He reached out to pull her into a big hug. "That long drive from Cody is getting old, though."

"I warned you," she said lightly, although her eyes darkened with concern. "If you've changed your mind..."

"I haven't." He kissed her. "Trust me, I love you. I love your family. And I'm sure I'll love my new job."

"I hope so." She frowned. "But what if you don't? What will you do?"

"Maya, I'll figure it out. I wouldn't be here if I didn't want to be." He kicked himself for complaining. He subtly patted his pocket. He'd wanted to propose at dinner, but her apprehension tugged at his heart. He almost tripped over Zion as he drew Maya into the living room. He faced her, then went down on one knee. Zion seemed to think it was a game, so she sat beside him. He smiled at the dog, hoping Zion would approve as he pulled the ring box from his pocket, opened it, and held it out to her. "Maya, I love you. Will you please marry me?"

"Marry you?" Her eyes widened with surprise. "I—but—we—"

"Love each other." He held her gaze. Zion bumped him with her nose as if to say hurry up. "We love each other, and while we both made mistakes by marrying the wrong person in the past, we're older and wiser now. We know what we want. And I want you. You should know I spoke to Chase. He was caught off guard when I asked for permission to marry you but gave us his blessing."

"You asked Chase?" Her eyebrows rose. "Really?"

"Yes. At first, he muttered something about not being your father, but then he gave me his seal of approval. I think the rest of the family likes me too." When she didn't say anything, he added, "But all that matters is you. I love you, Maya. I want you to be my wife. Will you please marry me?"

"Oh, Doug. Yes. Yes! I'll marry you." She tugged him upright and threw herself into his arms. "I love you so much."

He held her close as Zion's curvy tail thumped against his legs. Maya was a package deal, not only with Zion but with her younger brothers and sisters too. "Don't make me wait too long, okay?" he said into her hair. "There may not be a lot of traffic out here, but the commute is still brutal."

"That's what you meant," she said with a laugh. "Here I thought you were having doubts about moving to Wyoming."

"Never." He kissed her again. "This is where I belong. With you."

After a moment, she broke away and turned to the sofa. "Have a seat. I think there's something you should know."

"Oh yeah?" He pulled her down onto the sofa beside him. "Whatever it is, we can face it together."

Her expression softened. "That's very sweet. But this isn't exactly bad news. I, uh, may not have explained how the ranch is financed."

"You mean other than by donations of dog food?" he teased.

"Yes, like that." She sighed. "We have a significant inheritance that keeps us operationally solvent. It's one of the reasons we only accept dog food as a fee for service. The money is tied up in a trust that Chase and I manage together. We pay ourselves and the other siblings a modest salary, but most of the money goes into paying for the ranch, the horses and dogs, the equipment..." She waved a hand. "Everything."

He frowned, trying to understand. "The cost of running this place must be pretty significant."

"It is." She met his gaze. "You never struck me as someone swayed by money..."

"Hey, I completely understand. I'll sign a prenup, no problem," he hastened to reassure her. "I have a modest retirement account that I'll gladly share with you, but I don't need anything belonging to your family or the ranch. I just want you."

"Oh, Doug." Tears shone in her eyes, filling him with panic. Had he said the wrong thing? "I love you so much."

"And I love you." He breathed a sigh of relief. "That's all that matters, Maya. I only need your love. And maybe kids. If you're willing."

"I'd like that, if I'm not too old," she said.

"All the more reason to get married sooner than later." He grinned. "I'll find a lawyer to draw up a prenup. That shouldn't take too long, and once that's signed, we can—"

"No prenup." She lifted her hand. "It's sweet that you offered, and that alone tells me I've made the right choice in falling in love with you. But there's no need. I love you and trust you with my life. All I ask is that we live on the ranch. I'd like to be here to support my siblings."

Zion came over to rest her head on Maya's knee. He stroked Zion's fur. "I'd live anywhere with you. But I'm not joking about getting married soon." He drew her into his arms again. "We need to get started on having a family of our own."

"I can't wait," she whispered.

As they kissed and cuddled in front of the fire, Doug's heart swelled with anticipation for their future. Maya, Zion, and their children.

God's blessings of love.

I HOPE you enjoyed Maya and Doug's story! I'm already having fun writing about the Sullivan K9 Search and Rescue ranch. Are you ready to read about Chase Sullivan in *Scent of Panic*? Click here!

DEAR READER

Thanks for reading *Scent of Danger*! I hope you enjoyed Doug and Maya's story. I am having fun with this new Sullivan K9 Search and Rescue series. If you've been following my books for a while, you know how much I love dogs. These adorable and amazing K9s are the true heroes of these stories.

Don't forget, you can purchase ebooks or audiobooks directly from my website will receive a 15% discount by using the code **LauraScott15**.

I adore hearing from my readers! I can be found through my website at https://www.laurascottbooks.com, via Facebook at https://www.facebook.com/LauraScottBooks, Instagram at https://www.instagram.com/laurascottbooks/, and Twitter https://twitter.com/laurascottbooks. Please take a moment to subscribe to my YouTube channel at youtube.com/@LauraScottBooks-wr1xl?sub_confirmation=1. Also take a moment to sign up for my monthly newsletter to learn about my new book releases! All subscribers receive a free novella not available for purchase on any platform.

Until next time,
Laura Scott
PS: Read on for a sneak peek of *Scent of Panic*.

SCENT OF PANIC

Chapter One

Wynona Blackhorse headed up to the front door of her neighbor's home. Her job working as an accountant for the tribal council for the Shoshone Wind River Reservation didn't end until four thirty, and her four-and-a-half-year-old son, Eli, rode home from school with his 4-K preschool teacher, Shana Wildbloom, during the weekdays.

She knocked on the front door, then tried the door handle. Normally, Shana left it open for her, knowing she'd be there to pick up Eli.

The door was locked. She frowned, wondering what had caused Shana to do such a thing. A frisson of concern snaked down her spine. She listened intently for a moment but heard nothing. She knocked again, harder.

No answer. The clouds overhead made the temperature feel cooler than usual, even though it was a balmy thirty-two degrees. She didn't see any lights on inside either. When there was still no response to her third pounding, she moved to the window to press her face against the glass.

And gasped when she saw Shana lying on the floor, blood staining her temple.

"Shana! Eli!" She slammed her hands against the glass so hard she was surprised it didn't break. Then she ran around to the next window, hoping to see Eli. But every room she could see into appeared empty.

Raw panic clawed up her throat, sending her pulse into triple digits. She ran all the way around to the back door, nearly sobbing in relief when she realized that one wasn't locked. Bolting inside, she knelt beside Shana.

"Shana! Wake up!" She shook the young woman's shoulder. "It's Wyn. What happened? Where's Eli?"

"Wyn?" Shana's eyelids fluttered open, and she stared up at her in confusion. "Who hit me?"

"I don't know. I just arrived here to pick up Eli. What happened? Where's my son?" Sliding her arm behind Shana's shoulders, she helped her sit up.

"I—he was wearing a face mask." Shana put her hand to her temple, grimacing at the blood. "I was playing with Eli when he entered the house and struck me."

Wyn noticed the building blocks scattered across the floor and could imagine the young preschool teacher playing with Eli. She rose on shaky legs and began searching the home in earnest. Maybe Eli had been frightened by the intruder and had run away to hide. But even as she looked inside closets, under the beds, and behind doors, she knew the masked man had taken her son.

She quickly returned to the living room. "Did you see what kind of car he was driving?" Remaining calm wasn't easy, but she needed all the information from Shana that she could get. "Can you remember anything else about him?"

"He was tall and lean with dark-brown eyes." Shana closed her eyes for a moment. "Maybe a white pickup truck? I noticed one parked a few houses down the road but didn't think anything of it as we passed by."

The description wasn't very helpful, but she didn't take her anger and frustration out on her friend. Instead, she pulled her phone from her pocket and scrolled to a number she hadn't called in over five years. Drawing a steadying breath and willing her panic at bay, she waited for him to answer.

"Wynona?" The shocked surprise in Chase Sullivan's tone sent a chill over her. He was the last man she should call.

He was also the only man who could find her son.

Their son.

"Chase, I need help. My son is missing, and I need your K9 search and rescue expertise to search for him."

"Your son?" Again, there was no mistaking the shocked surprise. "I—didn't realize you were married."

"I'm not. I don't have time to discuss the details now, but I need you. I need you to head to the rez and help me find Elijah." After a pause, she added, "Please. I desperately need your help to find him."

"I'll be there as quickly as I can. In the meantime, I need you to gather several of your son's recently worn clothing together for my K9 Rocky to use as a scent source. Have you called the tribal police?"

"Not yet." Their police department was small and covered the entire reservation. She wasn't at all confident in their ability to find Eli.

"Make the call," Chase advised. "I'll be there as soon as

possible." His reassuring tone didn't make her feel any better. She had never been to his ranch, but she knew it was a good two-hour drive from her current location. "Where are you?"

"Riverton." She gave him the location; they didn't use typical addresses on the rez. Her throat thickened with fear and worry. "Please hurry."

"I'll do my best. Call me if anything changes."

"I will." She gripped the phone tightly, trying not to imagine her son being injured or dead, and added, "Thank you."

"See you soon." Chase ended the call.

She didn't wear the cross necklace Chase had given her over six years ago, but she lifted her eyes to the overcast sky desperately seeking the Lord's support and guidance. She lowered the phone and turned to see Shana sitting in a chair at the kitchen table, holding her head in her hands.

"I don't understand. Who could have done this?" Shana's voice was barely a whisper. "I know there's plenty of crime on the rez, but usually not something like this."

"I'll get you some ice." Battling a wave of helplessness, Wyn crossed to the freezer. After making an ice pack for the preschool teacher, she turned back to survey the room. There was no sign of Eli's coat, hat, mittens, and boots. She wanted to be relieved that the kidnapper didn't mean her son harm if he'd taken time to dress him for the weather, but she wasn't.

She also noticed Eli's stuffed black horse was missing too.

After making the call to the tribal police, who promised to send an officer to Shana's home, she debated if it would help to contact her father, Ogima Blackhorse, one of the tribal leaders of the Shoshone Reservation. Then she quickly decided against it.

Her father wouldn't provide the emotional support she needed right now. Their relationship had been strained over the last year, despite his giving her a job working for the tribal council. He wanted her to move away from Riverton, claiming the city had more non-Native American's than those born to the land. And he was right about that, as part of downtown Riverton was no longer officially a part of the reservation. But rather than move to a city within the rez, she had been thinking of a very different change. One that involved moving off the reservation completely to Cody, Cheyenne, or Laramie for Eli's sake. Her son had needs that the schools on the rez couldn't meet. She knew he needed to be enrolled in the public schools of Wyoming. That would mean getting another job, but she wanted her son to have the best education possible.

But that was a topic for another day. Right now, she needed answers to who had taken Eli and why.

She hurried back outside to scan the neighborhood for a sign of the white pickup truck. She headed down the street in the direction Shana would have taken to come home from school, but she didn't see any vehicles parked there.

It wasn't smart to pin her hopes on a glimpse of a white pickup, but that's all she had to work from. Describing the assailant as a tall, lean man with dark-brown eyes fit almost half the men on the rez.

The panic at knowing her son was out there alone with strangers was crippling. She abruptly turned and headed on foot toward her home that was two doors down from Shana's. She snagged her phone charger in case the masked kidnapper called with some sort of ransom demand, then continued down the hall to her son's room. It didn't take long to put Eli's dirty clothes from yesterday into a bag. The fact that his shirt was stained from their spaghetti dinner made tears fill her eyes.

Would the kidnappers feed Eli? Would they keep him warm and sheltered from the wind, cold, and snow?

Her knees buckled, and she bowed her head and began to pray.

"Lord Jesus, I know You died to save me. Please spare my son's life." For a moment, she wondered if she was being punished for her sins. For the mistakes she'd made. For the secrets she'd kept.

A sob welled in her throat. Was this her fault? Was her little boy suffering at the hands of strangers because of her?

A Bible verse flashed in her mind. *In whom we have redemption through his blood, even the forgiveness of sins (Colossians 1:14).*

Swallowing hard, she lifted her head willing the panic at bay. She'd learned about forgiveness of their sins. She needed to keep her faith in Jesus.

And in Chase's ability to find their son, before it was too late.

∼

QUESTIONS ROLLED through Chase Sullivan's mind as he drove his specially designed K9 SUV down the highway toward Riverton. Six months ago, he'd taken a very similar path to the rez. He'd searched for a lost child, then, too. Nausea churned in his belly. What if he had the same outcome this time? Rocky had found the child, but too late. The little girl had been found dead at the bottom of a ravine.

Chase couldn't bear the thought of failing to rescue a second child.

He pushed his speed as much as he dared considering he was pulling a trailer. He'd decided to bring two snow machines. He knew the reservation had acres and acres of open land with very limited road access. In many cases, the direct line between two places couldn't be traveled by car, only by four-wheelers in the summer and snowmobiles in winter.

Using the rearview mirror, he glanced at his K9 Rocky. The large male Norwegian Elkhound was stretched out in the back crate area, looking around with interest. Rocky's fluffy fur belied his name but matched the dog's temperament to a T. Elkhounds could be incredibly stubborn and independent, and while Chase insisted on being the alpha in their relationship, Rocky didn't always go along with the plan.

But Rocky was a good tracker and loved the snow as much if not more than Maya's husky, Zion. Rocky considered the search game a challenge, whereas Maya's Zion played to please her handler. They were both good at their jobs, while being different in temperament. And both dogs had their high, ridiculously curled tails that often made him smile.

He wasn't smiling now. He hadn't seen Wynona in a little over five years, since the plane crash that had killed his parents. At the time, he'd had his own business as a hunting and fishing guide. He'd met Wynona in the town of Lander where she'd worked. They'd hit it off, and he had fallen hard for her. He'd hoped to marry her, but her father had not given his permission. Before he could find a way to win Wynona's father over, his parents had died.

He'd sold off his half of the Wyoming Wilderness Guide

company to his partner David Cooksey to head home to the ranch. His oldest sister, Maya, had done the same thing, giving up her career in law enforcement and moving from Cheyenne. It had never been an option not to head home to support their seven younger siblings. The property had once been an exclusive dude ranch, but it had been Maya's idea to change it into a search and rescue operation. Their new mission was to honor their dead parents. The siblings had spent weeks trekking through the wooded mountains in the approximate location where their parents' plane had gone down, without finding anything. No sign of the plane or their parents' bodies.

Only after the devastating loss did they discover the extent of their parents' wealth. He and Maya had been named the executors of the Sullivan trust and worked with the lawyers to make sure the ranch and all their siblings would be cared for into the future. Soon all the siblings wanted to be a part of the search and rescue operation. The Sullivan K9 Search and Rescue ranch was born and continued to flourish over the years as they successfully ran missions that had garnered them plenty of attention.

Yet it bothered Chase that they'd never found their parents. And while summers were typically their busiest season, he and his siblings often used whatever breaks they had in their schedules to continue their search efforts.

The trip down memory lane was his way of justifying why he'd left Wynona behind over five years ago. And he'd tried to reach out to her several times without a response. He'd even gone back to the reservation to see her in person, but she'd moved, and he didn't know where she'd gone. He'd always intended to go back, to try again, but suddenly there were dozens of search and rescue operations that needed their expertise, and the weeks had stretched into months, which had stretched into years.

Even six months ago when he'd searched for the lost child, he'd anticipated running into her. But he hadn't. And since the outcome had been grim, he and Rocky hadn't lingered.

Deep down, he'd known Wynona must have found someone else; otherwise, she would have returned one of his dozens of calls. His messages had begged her to come visit him on the ranch, but she never did. Now that he knew about her son, he understood she'd moved on.

That she'd called him now was a testament to her level of desperation. He should have asked more questions about the child. Rocky was good, but he wasn't sure how they would find a toddler in these wintery conditions. He called her back using his hands-free function.

"Chase? Where are you?" Wyn's voice was tense.

"I should be there in thirty minutes. I need you to fill me in on what happened so we can get to work as soon as I arrive."

"Eli was with Shana, his preschool teacher. I came to pick him up after work and found Shana lying on the floor bleeding from a wound on her temple. She said a masked man came into her house and assaulted her." Wyn's voice thickened. "I searched the house, but Eli is gone, along with his coat, hat, boots, mittens, and his stuffed horse."

"Did Shana recognize the man who came inside?"

"No. She described him as tall, lean and with dark-brown eyes. His features were covered in a face mask." She paused, then added, "Shana noticed a white pickup truck parked along the side of the road when she drove home with Eli. There's no sign of it now, but I gave that information to the tribal police."

He hated to admit the situation sounded grim. "Okay, I'll be there soon. Send me a copy of the picture you provide the tribal police. Keep asking Shana questions. Witnesses often remember details later when the initial shock wears off." At least, that's what Maya had told him.

"I will. Please hurry." She ended the call before he could even answer.

By the time he pulled up in front of the home Wyn had described, his muscles were tense with fear. His phone had pinged with the incoming text of the little boy's photo, but he hadn't dared take his eyes off the road to look at it. Darkness was falling, and the lack of lighting on the reservation would make the upcoming search that much more difficult. Before he could slide out from behind the wheel, Wyn ran out to the car.

"Thanks for coming." Her dark eyes were wide with fear as she held up a plastic bag. "I have Eli's clothes."

"Okay." He released the back hatch, and Rocky immediately jumped down, then lowered his snout to stretch his back. "Rocky, come."

The elkhound eyed him for a moment, then trotted over with his head and tail up as if he were a king agreeing to meet with a peasant.

Chase put a hand on Wynona's arm. "Friend. This is a friend."

Rocky sniffed her feet, her hands and coat, then wagged his tail. The dog was friendly enough as long as he wasn't being ordered around.

"Good boy," Wynona whispered. Then she cleared her throat and looked up at him expectantly. "I spoke with the tribal police, and Shana gave her statement as well. Where will you and Rocky start?"

"Here, since this is the last place Eli was seen." He glanced down at his dog. "Give me a minute to prepare Rocky for work." He reached for the bag containing Eli's clothes, then headed toward the rear hatch. Thankfully, Rocky followed.

Chase quickly looped Rocky's vest over his torso and cinched it tight. Rocky's nose lifted to the air, already anxious to explore. He clipped on a utility belt that contained various items that may come in handy during a search. He had a handgun but decided against pulling that out now.

When he was ready, he filled a small collapsible bowl with water and offered it to the K9. Moistening the dog's mucus membranes enhanced their scenting ability and was a routine part of their searches. Rocky ignored the water, looking away. This was one of their little tussles that made Chase grind his teeth in frustration.

Giving up on the water, he opened the bag and held it for Rocky. "This is Eli." He was relieved to see Rocky buried his snout into the clothing. At least his stubborn K9 liked to work. "Eli," he repeated. Then he added excitement to his tone. "Are you ready? Are you ready to work? Search! Let's search for Eli!"

Rocky's tail wagged back and forth, and the dog didn't hesitate. Despite his dislike for being given orders, Rocky lifted his nose into the air and sniffed for several long seconds. Then he wheeled and trotted to the sidewalk leading up to the house.

Wynona ran forward to follow, but he grabbed her arm, holding her back.

"Don't interfere," he warned. "Stay back so Rocky has room to work."

Her expression hardened for a moment, but then she gave a jerky nod. "I understand."

He offered what he hoped was a reassuring smile. This situation was different than the search six months ago. If Wynona knew how that one had turned out, she didn't let on. "Don't worry, Rocky is very good at his job."

On cue, the elkhound sat at the front door and gave a sharp bark. That was Rocky's alert. He wasn't quiet about it the way Zion and some of the other dogs were.

"Good boy," he praised but didn't offer the red ball as a reward. "Search for Eli!"

Rocky whirled, sniffed along the sidewalk again, this time trotting to the road. When his K9 partner turned to keep going, he hastened to follow. Wynona's concern radiated off her, but she stayed where she was.

Chase was surprised when Rocky went a good sixty yards down the road before stopping to sniff a particular area with interest. He stayed back, waiting for Rocky's signal.

It came a second later. The dog sat and let out a sharp bark.

"Is that a real alert?" Wyn asked, her voice shaky. "Does your dog believe Eli was there?"

"Yes, that's exactly what Rocky is telling us." He pulled a flashlight from his belt and carefully approached the location, playing the light over the street. There wasn't any fresh snow covering the ground; the road must have been plowed or shoveled since the last snowfall. But he paused when he noticed several footprints in the snow along the side of the road.

He drew the red rubber ball from his pocket and tossed it for Rocky. The dog loved playing with the ball and took off running, his curvy tail wagging from side to side.

Lowering to a crouch, he examined the footprints. As a hunting and fishing guide, he was more familiar with small and large game animal tracks than with human footwear. There was a partial tread left in the snow that matched a popular brand of outdoor boots that probably eighty percent of all men wore out here.

He didn't see a smaller footprint that may have belonged to Eli. He slowly rose and glanced back over his shoulder. Wyn was closer now, as if she was unable to stay away.

"Maybe you should take a look." He gestured for her to come closer. "Do you see any footprints that may belong to your son?"

She rushed forward and bent to examine the ground illuminated by his flashlight. The excitement in her expression quickly faded. "No. I don't see anything other than adult-sized boot prints, and those are crisscrossed, making it impossible to judge the size of the shoe."

He nodded. "That was my impression too. I have to assume your son was carried here, maybe set down briefly before being placed in the car."

"The white pickup truck," she whispered. "I think the driver of the truck waited here for Shana and Eli to arrive. Once he was convinced they were settled in, he pulled on his face mask and headed inside to grab my son."

It was a logical theory to a point. "Okay, do you have any idea why someone would take your son?"

"No, I've been racking my brain ever since I found out he was missing." Her voice hitched. "He's just a little boy. I don't understand what's going on!"

He watched as Rocky ran around with the ball in his mouth, then turned to face her. "Come on, Wyn. The obvious answer is that this is a custody dispute. Don't you think it's possible the child's father has come back for him?"

"No! This isn't about Eli's father." Her voice was so vehement he was taken aback. "I don't know why Eli has been taken. I've been waiting for a call for some sort of ransom demand, but there's been nothing!"

He frowned. "How do you know for sure the boy's father isn't the one who took him? The fact that there hasn't been a ransom demand means this is personal. And I can't think of anything more personal than a father who might be making a desperate move to be a part of his son's life."

"You don't know what you're talking about." She spat the words bitterly.

He sighed, striving for patience. "Okay, then help me understand. Because I'm getting the feeling that there's something you're not telling me."

She turned and stared off into the distance. Then she finally turned back to face him. "The reason I know this isn't a custody issue is because you are Eli's biological father."

The blood drained from his face. He was the boy's father? A wave of anger hit hard. He grabbed her shoulders, barely managing not to shake her senseless. "I'm his father? Why am I just hearing this now? Why didn't you tell me back when you discovered you were pregnant?"

Her eyes glittered with tears, but she didn't fight to pull away. She simply stared at him. "That's not important now. Eli is missing, and we need to work together to find him."

He tightened his grip, then abruptly released her. He grabbed his phone and opened the picture she'd sent earlier. A solemn-faced little boy stared back at him. He had his mother's dark hair and eyes, but Chase could see his chin in the boy's features.

He turned away, battling his anger. His son! He had a son! Yet he knew she was right. This wasn't the time to rehash the past. He could hate her for what she'd done, but that wasn't going to help.

The son he didn't know he had was missing. And other than a partial boot print and tire tracks that likely belonged to a white pickup truck, he had no idea how to find him.

Made in United States
North Haven, CT
15 February 2025